Weathering the Storms of Love . . .

S he couldn't make sense of her own feelings, either. Barnaby was sullen and insulting to her, yet knowing this, she was still drawn to him. The contradictions in her feelings were epitomized by her reactions to that kiss, at first so infuriating and later so . . . so overwhelming. She would have clung to him forever if he'd continued to hold her so.

But he hadn't continued. He'd made another of his abrupt mood changes. Cold and distant, he'd stalked away, leaving her shaken and confused. And shaken and confused she remained.

In the last analysis, however, the matter was so confusing. If one faced it honestly, it was quite simple. She could state the problem in fewer than ten words: *I'm in love with a man who despises me.*

Winter Wonderland

Elizabeth Mansfield

JOVE BOOKS, NEW YORK

WINTER WONDERLAND

A Jove Book/published by arrangement with
the author

PRINTING HISTORY
Jove edition/November 1993

ISBN: 0-515-11234-8

A JOVE BOOK®
Jove Books are published by The Berkley Publishing Group,
200 Madison Avenue, New York, New York 10016.
JOVE and the "J" design are trademarks belonging to Jove Publications, Inc.

PRINTED IN THE UNITED STATES OF AMERICA

10 9 8 7 6 5 4 3 2 1

· Prologue ·

BARNABY TRAHERNE, A tall, gawky nineteen-year-old, stood at the entrance of the ballroom of Lord Lydell's town house and stared inside in horror. The cacophony of loud voices and loud music was alarming enough, but the crush of people within was worse than anything he'd imagined. "I never should have come," he muttered in dismay.

Honoria, the Countess of Shallcross, who stood at his right, glanced up at her young brother-in-law worriedly. "Are you uneasy, my dear?" she asked kindly. "I know I would be, if this were *my* first ball."

On her other side, her husband, although twenty years older than Barnaby and with the experience of hundreds of balls behind him, did not look any happier than his brother. "What a crush!" he exclaimed in disgust. "I'd wager there are a hundred and fifty fools crowded into this room—a space designed to hold no more than sixty!"

"Then let's turn tail and go home," Barnaby urged, taking a backward step, quite ready to bolt.

Honoria grasped her husband's arm. "Perhaps, my love, the boy is right. We should go. His first ball should not be—"

But the butler was announcing their presence in a loud voice, and their hostess, Lady Lydell, was waving to them from the far side of the room.

"We *must* stay," the Earl reminded her. "We have social obligations. How can we consider making an escape when this misbegotten affair is in my honor?" He took a firm hold of his brother's arm and pulled him over the threshold. "Barnaby, try to look a little less alarmed. It's only a ball, after all."

But to the young Barnaby Traherne, who was truly, achingly, awkwardly, utterly shy, this was not "only" a ball. It was, in its way, a battlefield. He saw it as a test of his manhood, a test which, he belatedly realized, he was not yet prepared to face.

His brother, he knew, would not understand. It was hard for Lawrence Traherne, who'd lately come into his titles as the fourth Earl of Shallcross, to comprehend the feelings of a brother twenty years younger. Barnaby's father, the third Earl of Shallcross, had had four sons, of whom Barnaby was the youngest. Ten years separated him from his next-youngest brother, Harry. Because their mother had died shortly after Barnaby's first birthday, and the old Earl had been too bored with fatherhood to trouble himself with the newest baby, the brothers had taken it upon themselves to raise him. Though boisterous and domineering, they were also good-natured and kind, and they were delighted with this new responsibility. During all his formative years, Barnaby was cosseted and mollycoddled by three overprotective brothers and one motherly sister-in-law, Lawrence's wife Honoria.

During the years of his growing up, Barnaby had never been permitted to fight his own battles. One of the four was always on hand to defend him from any real or imagined attack. Even when he was a student at Oxford, one or another of his brothers managed to drop round often enough to keep a protective eye on him. The attention of his siblings was so pervasive that Barnaby's self-confidence could not properly develop. With so much custodial care, he was never permitted to stand up in his own defense, test his own courage, or even finish his own sentences. Shyness was the natural outcome. It was only recently that he'd begun to assert himself. Now, at nineteen, having won his degree and having returned from Oxford, it was finally time, he told himself, to fight his own battles.

This, however, was a battle he was not yet ready for. He should never have succumbed to Honoria's blandishments. She'd often tried to entice him to accompany them to the festivities being held in honor of the new Earl, but Barnaby had resisted her appeals with implacable resolve. "I'm not comfortable at social affairs," he told her. "I'm tongue-tied in the presence of elegant females, I'm an awkward dancer, and, furthermore, I don't own a decent set of evening clothes."

But yesterday, on the evening before the Lydell ball, he changed his mind. His brother Harry had spent the dinner hour bragging about the opera dancers and lightskirts with whom he'd been successful. The stories had filled young Barnaby with envy, for he himself had no experience of Womanhood. Moreover, it was a night when the air was fragrant and the moon cast a silver glow on all the world. What man could ignore the magnetic appeal of the female with such suggestive reminders all around him? Barnaby, feeling the blood of youth and health coursing through his veins, felt impelled to act. He admitted to his sister-in-law that he yearned to hold a pretty young woman in his arms. "So if you wish, Honoria," he said in blushing surrender, "I'll go with you to your ball tomorrow."

Honoria, delighted at this turn of events, set about at once to see that her brother-in-law was properly turned out. With an evening coat borrowed from Harry's wardrobe, trousers from Terence's, and a lace-trimmed neckcloth and striped satin waistcoat from the collection of the Earl himself, she and Lawrence's valet managed to outfit him. Barnaby, studying himself in the mirror, suspected that the waistcoat hung too loosely about his chest even after being taken in at the back, and that the sleeves of Harry's coat were a bit too short, but Honoria, looking him over with affectionate eyes, declared firmly that his appearance was perfectly satisfactory.

Now, however, standing here in the ballroom doorway and eyeing all those well-dressed men within, poor Barnaby was suddenly filled with misgivings. Moreover, the noise of the milling throng within was an assault on his senses. The nine musicians sawing away on their strings were no match for the chatter and laughter that reverberated through the room. Not only were one's ears assaulted but one's eyes. It was a scene of glinting, confusing movement: glasses clinked, jewels twinkled in the light of three enormous chandeliers, footmen maneuvered their way through the crowd carrying trays of canapes over their heads, and one hundred and fifty ladies and gentlemen jostled for space and attention. The turmoil made Barnaby wince. The impulse that had made him wish to attend this affair immediately vanished. All he wanted now was to shake himself loose from his brother's hold and break for the door. It had been stupid to come, he berated himself. He should never have agreed to—

But at that moment, his attention was caught by a scene at his left. He could not have missed it, for it took place on a staircase-landing in the far corner, a landing raised three steps above the level of the ballroom floor like the stage in a theater. On that raised landing, in the midst of a clutch of admirers, a young woman had just thrown her head back in laughter.

Barnaby blinked. His Adam's apple bobbed as he took in a gulp of air. The sound of that laughter was attractive enough all by itself—a light, musical laugh that tinkled above the noise with the crystalline clarity of a glass bell— but it was the *appearance* of the lady that held his attention once it was caught. She was the most beautiful creature he'd ever beheld. Tall and lithe, draped in green silk that clung to every curve of breast, hip and thigh, she took his breath away. Her skin gleamed, and her auburn hair glinted with gold in the light of the chandelier above her head. And at this moment, her throat, stretched taut by the angle of her head and pulsing with laughter, looked so lovely it caused a clench of pain in Barnaby's chest. He was smitten, as only a very young man can be. "Who *is* she?" he croaked as soon as he could manage his voice.

The Earl grinned broadly. "Why, that's Miranda Pardew!" he chortled. "You've got taste, Barnaby, I'll say that for you."

"Good God, she's lovely," Barnaby breathed.

"No argument there. She's a distant cousin of ours, you know. Would you like to meet her?"

Honoria threw her husband a look of alarmed disapproval. "Meet her? Are you mad?" she demanded.

"Why?" the Earl asked his wife, befuddled. "Why shouldn't he—?"

"Do you want the boy eaten alive? Miranda Pardew is not the right sort for Barnaby. Not at all. Why, this is only her second season, and she's already earned a reputation. During her first, she jilted two men and caused a third to take monastic vows. Is that the sort of girl you want to introduce to our Barnaby?"

Barnaby, his eyes still fixed on the breathtaking creature, hardly heard what his sister-in-law was saying. "Look at her," he sighed, entranced. "She can smile with only her eyes!"

Honoria rolled her eyes heavenward. "Listen to me, Lawrence," she hissed in her husband's ear. "My friends tell me that Miss Pardew has rejected more than a dozen offers of marriage and set her cap for Sir Rodney Velacott. He's the fellow, you know, who's bragged for years that he'll never succumb to matrimony. The betting book at White's has set odds of nine to one that 'the Magnificent Miranda'—yes, that's what they call her!—will manage to catch him. And Sir Rodney is standing right up there beside her. Look at him in that circle of her admirers, looking smug! With that fish to fry, Miranda Pardew will take no interest in Barnaby! He should be meeting a sweet, quiet girl who'd fawn on him, not a heartless flibbertigibbet who'll toss him aside like an old shoe!"

"I only want him to dance with her," the Earl retorted, "not marry her."

Honoria turned to her brother-in-law. "Barnaby, my dear," she said in what seemed to Barnaby to be real distress, "Miss Pardew is not the sort—"

But before she could finish, their hostess, having successfully made her way through the press, came up to them. Showering them with effusive greetings, she linked her arm to Honoria's and, without giving her a chance to object, bore her off to make the social rounds. Barnaby saw Honoria look over her shoulder worriedly, as if she wanted to warn him of something, but before she could make herself heard, she was swallowed up by the crowd.

His brother, however, showed no such distress. "Come, boy," he said, his grin reappearing as he took his brother's arm, "and let me introduce you to that charming creature who has you gawking. Don't pay any attention to Honoria's gossip."

Barnaby blinked at his brother in trepidation. "*Introduce* me?" he asked, so frightened at the prospect of having to speak to the dazzling creature that he almost stuttered.

"Of course. Don't gape at me like a frightened fish. I'll introduce you, and then you will ask her to dance."

"Dance?" Barnaby echoed. "But I don't—"

"Of course you do," his brother interrupted as he always did. "Nothing to it." And, dragging poor Barnaby behind him, he moved inexorably toward the platform where the ravishing young woman stood. "Miss Pardew," he bellowed as soon as they were in earshot, not at all concerned that he might be interrupting the young woman in the midst of an important flirtation, "how do ye do?"

The girl looked round, her smile fading and her expression becoming guarded—a look often seen in the eyes of mischievous young people in the presence of their elders. "Lord Shallcross, good evening," she said. If she was annoyed at the interruption, she did not reveal it by so much as a blink. "How kind of you, the guest of honor, to come out of your way to greet me."

"Not kind at all," his lordship replied, stepping up on the landing, breaking in on her circle of admirers and lifting her hand to his lips. "I feel it a family obligation to greet you. After all, you are a relation to me, did you know that?"

"Yes, I'd heard something of the sort," the girl acknowledged, her charming smile reappearing. "I do believe we're cousins, though quite distant."

The Earl nodded. "Your father was my second cousin once removed, if I calculate rightly."

Sir Rodney, who'd been standing behind the girl, moved closer to her. "A second cousin once removed, is he?" he muttered in Miranda's ear. "I only wish he'd remove himself further."

The lovely Miss Pardew could not quite restrain her giggle as she dropped Lord Shallcross a curtsey.

Lawrence chose to ignore Sir Rodney's obvious rudeness. "I'd like to make this young man known to you, my dear," he said to the lady pleasantly. "He is just out of Oxford and therefore somewhat tongue-tied. I believe he has a request to make of you." In his blunt, fatherly style, he pulled Barnaby up on the landing and pushed him toward the girl. "Go on, boy! Ask her!" he ordered. Then, bestowing a benign smile on both of them, he stepped down from the landing and walked off, abandoning poor Barnaby to his fate.

Barnaby felt himself redden to the ears as the girl looked him over with cool disdain, taking in his unkempt hair, ill-fitting coat and loose breeches in one disparaging glance. "What can you possibly wish to ask me, sir?"

Barnaby, more humiliated than he'd ever been in his life, could barely find his tongue. "I w-w-wondered, Miss P-Pardew," he managed, "if I might have the n-n-next dance."

"Next dance? What gall!" exclaimed one of the men surrounding the lady. "I should say not! Her dance card was filled more than an hour ago!"

"I can speak for myself, Charlie," the lady scolded, tapping the offending gentleman on his knuckles with her fan. Then she turned back to Barnaby. "Did no one ever tell you, young man, that asking a lady to dance at the very last moment can—in certain situations—be considered an insult?"

"An insult?" Barnaby was sincerely bewildered. "I don't see how—"

"Don't you? One asks one's maiden aunt to dance at the last moment. Or one's little sister. Or a wallflower one feels sorry for. Do I look like someone's maiden aunt? Or a wallflower?"

Barnaby, completely at a loss, shifted his weight from one foot to the other. "Well," he muttered miserably, "I didn't . . . I wasn't . . . I just . . ."

"You didn't. You weren't. You just," she mocked. "A man of few words, eh?"

The men around her laughed loudly. Never had Barnaby felt such a fool.

Sir Rodney put a proprietary arm about the young lady's waist. "What the lady means, you young idiot," he said with a pitying smile, "is that she is spoken for already. The next dance is mine."

"I'm s-sorry," Barnaby stammered, backing away awkwardly. "P-Perhaps some other—" His voice, like his self-esteem, faded away to nothing.

The girl seemed to enjoy his misery. "For a man of few words," she taunted, "you do keep tripping over them."

"Yes, m—" he began, but his sentence was cut off by a loss of balance; he'd backed to the edge of the landing and stumbled off the edge. He lurched backwards down the three steps, not quite falling but merely looking like a clumsy ass.

The girl looked down at him as he steadied himself, her brows arched in amusement. "You not only trip over your words, but your feet. What a delicious combination of gracelessness and gaucherie!"

There was another roar of laughter from the gentlemen, but Miss Pardew merely smiled. Nevertheless, Barnaby could see that she was enjoying herself. She seemed to find it amusing to turn a man into a fool. Barnaby was not so green that he didn't recognize her delight in flaunting her power over him, and in having Sir Rodney witness that power.

Barnaby blinked up at her, wondering how to end this torture. No longer did she seem beautiful or desirable. The only desire he felt was an urgent wish to be gone from her presence. "Excuse my p-presumption, ma'am," he said, making a quick but clumsy bow. "I obviously made a mistake. I wish you g-good evening."

But she was not yet through with him. "I would wish you good evening in return, sir, but it seems I've forgotten your name. Or did Lord Shallcross fail to give it to me? What *is* your name, fellow?"

Barnaby had the urge to tell her to take a damper. To cut line. To cease her gibble-gabble. His brothers would not hesitate to say those things. *Rudeness*, he wished he had the courage to retort, *is only weakness masquerading as strength.*

"Did you hear me, fellow?" she persisted. "What is your name?"

He stared up at her, tongue-tied. What did she want with his name anyway? To use it as the subject for her mirth after he was gone? *Never mind my name*, his mind said silently. *I only want to say that this meeting was a pleasure—if not in the arrival, at least in the departure.* But overwhelmed with shyness and humiliation as he was, he was incapable of defending himself in any way, of paying her in kind, or even of making that mild rejoinder. He could only answer helplessly, "My name is Bar—"

But she held up a restraining hand. "No. On second thought, don't tell me. Please don't give me your name." She flipped the upraised hand in a gesture of airy rejection. "I'd rather dismiss you *incognito*."

The onlookers roared at this riposte. And the lady, having reduced the poor fellow to quivering jelly, was now ready to return her attention to Sir Rodney, her main objective. She turned away at last, leaving Barnaby free to make his escape. As he pushed his way through the crowd, he could hear her tinkling laughter as it merged with the hoots of hilarity the others were expelling at his expense.

He got through the rest of the evening somehow, and later, at home, he sat down in front of the sitting room fire to think over the event. The evening had been a battle, just as he'd anticipated. And he'd lost it. He had to admit that. He'd lost it ignominiously.

He stared at the dying fire, experiencing the humiliation of defeat. But he didn't wallow in mortification for long. He was too young and too hardheaded, he decided, to let one defeat overwhelm him. There were many battles of the sexes still ahead of him. He would enter the fray again, and the next time he would be better prepared. *The war's not over yet*, he said to himself, squaring his shoulders. *Not by a long shot!*

· One ·

HONORIA, LADY SHALLCROSS, had a select circle of friends—like herself, refined, mature ladies of impeccable taste and breeding—who gathered in her drawing room weekly to do what ladies of such refinement are wont to do: drink tea and gossip. And one of their favorite subjects of gossip was Honoria's own brother-in-law, Barnaby Traherne. What made him interesting was the paradoxical fact that, although he was tall, handsomely featured, and reasonably well-to-do, none of the marriageable young ladies of the *ton* seemed inclined to set their caps for him.

The subject became almost heated one day when Honoria, pouring out the tea for the large-bosomed Lady Lydell, chanced to remark that this was Barnaby's thirtieth birthday.

"It's positively shocking," Lady Lydell observed, helping herself to a buttered scone, "that such a catch as Barnaby is, at his age, still a bachelor."

"I don't understand it," the white-haired Jane Ponsonby mused. "The girls should be pursuing him relentlessly. Why aren't they?"

"Because," Honoria replied in that tone of unalterable affection with which she always spoke of him, "he's shy."

This response brought forth a burst of satiric laughter. "Shy, indeed!" the sharp-tongued Molly Davenham,

Honoria's closest friend, exclaimed. "The man's as shy as a shark!"

Honoria stiffened. "Molly! How *can* you say such a thing?" she demanded furiously.

"I can say it because it's true." Molly stirred her tea with perfect calm. "A man with a stinging wit can't be called shy."

"And didn't he win a DSO for his bravery at Waterloo?" Jane Ponsonby asked. "Hardly the act of a shy man."

"But . . . but that doesn't mean—" Honoria sputtered.

"I heard, from my nephew in the Foreign Office," Lady Lydell cut in, "that your Barnaby is the only man there with the backbone to stand up to the Prime Minister. So how can he be shy?"

Honoria brushed back a lock of gray-streaked hair with fingers that shook with anger. "Nevertheless—"

"Never mind your neverthelesses," Molly Davenham said bluntly. "The fact is that every young lady I've tried to push in Barnaby's path was afraid of him."

"*Afraid* of him?" Honoria stared at her friend in disbelief. "What on earth can have made them afraid of him?"

"He's forbidding," Molly said, reaching for a cucumber sandwich, "and if you can't see that for yourself, I can't help you."

"Forbidding? *My* Barnaby, *forbidding?*" Honoria looked round the circle for support for her position, but there was none.

"I know what Molly means," Lady Lydell said thoughtfully, "although perhaps it's hard to describe just what it is that makes him forbidding. . . ."

It *was* hard to describe, but everyone who knew him agreed that there was something about Barnaby Traherne that put one off. He had a strong, lean face and a body that showed not an ounce of self-indulgence, qualities not necessarily daunting in themselves (in fact, most females found him quite attractive), but when combined with a certain glower in his expression, forbidding he became. His dark eyes, which glittered with saturnine intellectual acumen, had a way of cutting through a lady's pretensions; his manner of responding to most questions with brusque monosyllables quickly exhausted most ladies' efforts at conversation; and his icy witticisms easily discouraged the most persistent of flirts. And though his normal expression was only mildly thoughtful, the least annoyance caused it to give way to a frown so glowering that most observers backed out of range.

But Honoria, who had no children of her own and who'd helped raise Barnaby since he was ten, saw the man with a loving mother's eyes. "What nonsense!" she insisted sternly. "My Barnaby is as shy as a wallflower. You may take my word on it."

But none of the ladies took her word. They all had eyes and ears, and from the evidence of those most reliable of organs, Barnaby Traherne was anything but shy.

Honoria didn't pursue the subject, though she knew how wrong they were. There was much they didn't know about her Barnaby, but his story was not one which she wished to tell, even to these close friends. *If only you could have seen him as I did,* she sighed to herself as she sipped her tea, *eleven years ago, back in 1806, when he attended his first ball . . . that dreadful ball that altered his character forever. . . .*

Honoria remembered that ball better than she remembered her own wedding. It was one of those affairs given to honor her husband's coming into his titles. After a year of mourning for his father, Lawrence Traherne, the fourth Earl of Shallcross, was ready to celebrate his new position. It was a happy time, a time of celebration in the family, for not only had their year of mourning come to an end, but Terence, the second brother, had become father to a bouncing boy, and Barnaby, who'd been an excellent student despite his shyness, had won his Oxford degree with honors.

To celebrate, Lawrence had taken the whole family to London for a season of gaiety. Many of the *ton* held fêtes for the new Earl. During that season, Honoria had often tried to entice the shy young Barnaby to accompany them to the festivities being held in his brother's honor, but Barnaby had been too shy to go. This time, however, something had made him change his mind.

Honoria was delighted. She'd looked forward to this particular affair, for it was being given by her good friends, Lord and Lady Lydell. She remembered how excited she'd been as she'd climbed the stairs of the Lydell town house in Portman Square, her husband holding her right arm, and Barnaby, her left.

But as soon as they approached the ballroom doorway, Honoria was struck with misgivings. Perhaps she shouldn't have urged Barnaby to come. Honesty demanded she admit to herself that she'd not thought things through. She'd been too eager, too hasty. Barnaby would not be presented at his best. There had not been time to prepare him properly. He'd not been schooled in ballroom etiquette; he'd not been warned of the many social pitfalls; he'd not even been dressed to advantage. The boy's hair had not been cut, his borrowed coat now seemed a poor fit, and his breeches positively baggy when compared with the exquisite tailoring exhibited by the other guests. *This is all my fault*, she berated herself. *I should not have permitted him to attend his very first ball so ill-prepared.*

She could sense that poor Barnaby, too, was beset with doubts, though not from the flaws in his costume or the gaps in his education, for he was too naive to be aware of them, but from the shyness that was so much part of his character. But Lawrence pulled him into the ballroom before she could prevent it. And before they'd had a chance to adjust to the noise, Barnaby spotted Miranda Pardew!

Honoria, following his gaze, felt her heart sink. Right before her eyes, the boy became bewitched. She could not blame him; the laughing young woman attracted the eye of many of the gentlemen present. But of all the women in the room, this one was the last she would have chosen for her shy, inexperienced brother-in-law.

But her husband, with typical male ineptitude in these matters, would not heed her warnings. Before she could persuade him to change his intent, Lady Lydell came up to them, linked her arm to Honoria's and, without giving her a chance to object, bore her off to make the social rounds. As she moved away, the last words Honoria could hear were her husband's: "Come, boy," he was saying, "and let me introduce you to that charming creature who has you gawking."

Honoria had wanted to wring his neck. She kept looking back over her shoulder, wishing urgently that she could find a way to keep her husband from throwing Barnaby to the mercy of the room's most notorious flirt. But her hostess's strong grip was irresistible. She tried to signal her alarm to Lawrence by means of meaningful glances, but the Earl did not receive his lady's mental messages. He merely pushed the boy onward to what Honoria feared would be certain disaster.

Later, at home, after everyone in the household had gone to bed, Honoria learned how right her feelings had been. She came downstairs to find Barnaby brooding before the embers of the sitting room fire. With gentle prodding, she drew the story out of him. It moved her to tears. "Oh, my poor, sweet boy, how dreadful! That you should have had to experience such a set-down . . . and at your very first ball . . . it breaks my heart!"

But Barnaby was past self-pity. "Don't cry over the incident, Honoria," he said to her, his jaw set and his eyes dark with resolve. "It won't happen to me again. When next I set foot in society, I shall be fully prepared."

And so he was. No sign of shyness ever again appeared in his demeanor. He conquered that tendency so completely that now, eleven years later, none of the ladies drinking tea with Honoria would believe that the word *shy* could possibly apply to him.

Honoria looked up from her reverie to find Jane Ponsonby staring at her speculatively. "Well?" she was asking.

"Well, what?" Honoria blinked at her in confusion, not having heard a word.

"Well, do you think Barnaby would like her?"

"Like who?"

"Dash it, Honoria, haven't you heard *anything*?" Molly Davenham asked in disgust. "Your habit of drifting off is becoming positively distressing. Jane was speaking of her niece, Olivia. Do you think Barnaby might take to her?"

"Little Livy?" Honoria looked from one to the other in surprise. "But she's much too young, isn't she? A mere child."

"She's twenty-two," Jane Ponsonby declared, "and has been out three seasons."

"Has she really? How time does fly! But how did you come to think of her as suitable for Barnaby?"

"Because of what you said about him, insisting that the fellow is shy. So is Livy. If she weren't, she'd have been spoken for years ago, pretty thing that she is. Three seasons on the town and the chit still hangs back behind her mother's skirts. She's perfectly charming and talkative at home, but bring her to a ballroom, and she barely utters a word!"

"It might be a perfect pairing," Lady Lydell cooed, her eyes alight with a matchmaker's gleam.

Molly Davenham, however, was not a romantic. "I don't see how it can be done, with Barnaby so put-offish and Livy so shy."

"I do," said Honoria, already smiling dreamily at the prospect of a bride for her darling Barnaby. "I know just how to manage it."

"How?" asked the skeptical Molly.

"The family will all be meeting at Terence's place for Christmas. I'll simply bring Livy with me. At a quiet family gathering in the country, we can all relax and be ourselves. No one need worry about being shy."

The ladies all smiled at each other over their cups. Not even Molly could think of an objection. And as for Honoria, her heart actually sang in her chest. Olivia Ponsonby, little

Livy, was just the sort of girl Honoria had wished for Barnaby all those years ago at the Lydell ball: a girl who was sweet, modest, pretty and shy! Livy had come along eleven years late, but better late than never.

Honoria lifted her cup in a toast. "To sweet little Livy!" she said happily.

"To sweet little Livy," the others echoed.

"May she have success," Molly added wryly, "where braver girls have failed."

· *Two* ·

MIRANDA, LADY VELACOTT, looked most unladylike sitting on the dining room floor. She was swathed in an oversized apron and employed in wrapping pieces of china in sheets of old newspaper. It was an unusual occupation for a lady, but Miranda had long since grown accustomed to performing menial tasks. In a household that had once been run by a dozen servants but which had for a long time been reduced in staff to only three, she'd learned that her title did not protect her from having to engage in such unladylike but necessary tasks as bedmaking, laundering, mending, cooking and dusting.

A few feet away from Miranda, kneeling in front of two wooden crates into which she was carefully placing the wrapped dishes, was her Aunt Letty, a bony, spare, aristocratic old woman with small black eyes, a beak-like nose and a smooth helmet of iron-gray hair, all of which gave the impression of a silver-headed bird. Miranda, in her shapeless apron and with her curly auburn hair falling in neglected disarray around her shoulders, made a sharp contrast to her formally-clad, neatly-coiffed aunt.

The younger woman, her head lowered and her falling hair shading her face, was carefully keeping her back to her aunt. By hiding her face, Miranda hoped the sharp-eyed old woman would not notice that she was crying again. She couldn't seem to keep from dripping tears today. The sight of the familiar blue willow pattern on the Minton china reminded her of the many soothing cups of tea she'd taken in Letty's company during the past eleven years in this London house. Through those long years of her disastrous marriage, the companionship of this honest, blunt, sensible yet affectionate woman—who'd been like a mother to her after her parents died—was her one blessing, her bulwark against life's storms, the lifeline that kept her from drowning. The thought that this was their last day together was too hard to bear.

But Aunt Letty was indeed sharp-eyed. "You are not working, my dear," she said, eyeing her niece's back suspiciously. "Don't tell me you've turned on the waterworks again."

Miranda surreptitiously wiped her eyes. "No, of course I haven't," she said bravely. "I was only . . ." Her mind raced about, searching for an excuse for her idle hands. " . . . only noticing something in the newspaper here."

"Were you indeed?" Letty was too shrewd to be easily fooled. "And what on earth can interest you in a newspaper so old that it's good for nothing but wrapping?"

Miranda looked desperately at the printed sheet she had half-folded over a pretty saucer. "Advertisements," she said with false brightness. "Have you ever read these advertisements, my love? Did you know that ladies of quality actually use newspapers to find themselves household help? Here's a Lady Millington in Kent seeking 'a well-qualified butler with experience in supervision of household staff of more than two dozen.' Two dozen! Imagine! And here . . . a family in Norfolk by the name of Traherne seeks 'the assistance of a gentlewoman to supervise and educate three boys, ages five through twelve.' And this one, from a Mr. Drinkwater in Essex for 'a gentleman's gentleman, skilled at hairdress—' "

"Thank you, my dear, that's quite enough. You may find such reading interesting, but I do not. Besides, did you not insist that we pack these crates before I take my leave?"

"Sorry, Aunt," Miranda said, making a last brush at her cheek with the back of her hand and hurrying on with the wrapping, "but we have all afternoon. We'll finish in time."

A sound of wheels on the gravel drive outside the windows caught their attention. "Goodness me, Higgins can't have brought my carriage round so soon!" Aunt Letty exclaimed, raising herself to her feet with the stiff awkwardness of age. Once on her feet, however, she scurried to the window with the agility of a much younger woman and peered out. "Heavens, that's not my carriage! It's a drayman's cart! Those blasted Velacotts have sent their things!"

"Already?" Miranda felt her heart sink.

Aunt Letty frowned in irritation. "Isn't it just like your brother-in-law and his grasping little wife to take over the house a day early?"

Miranda rose and joined her at the window. "It's their right," she said, trying to keep her voice steady. "At least they gave me a year's mourning before moving in."

Letty snorted. "How very good of them."

They stood in the window, arms about each other's waists, listening to the November wind rattle the panes. The draymen down below ignored the wind as they busily carried furniture and boxes from the equipage and piled them up in the drive. Letty leaned closer to the window, her birdlike eyes glittering in disgust as she watched them. "I suppose this means that the Charles Velacotts themselves will be following shortly."

Miranda winced at the prospect. "Oh, dear, I suppose they will. I had hoped for one more night . . ."

Aunt Letty threw her niece a quick look of sympathy before turning away from the window and starting across the room. "Then I'd best send Higgins for the carriage and take myself off before they arrive."

"Yes, I suppose you sh-should," Miranda said, her voice choking on the tears she was trying desperately to control. "I know you don't wish to f-face them."

Letty, hearing the catch in Miranda's voice, stopped in her tracks. She'd made up her mind to keep her emotions in strict restraint during this final hour, but her strength failed her. She turned back to her niece, her eyes filling with the tears she'd promised herself not to shed. "Oh, my dearest," she cried, taking Miranda's hands in hers, "don't look so! Come with me to Cousin Hattie. We shall manage somehow."

Miranda shook her head. "We've been over this too many times to have to remind ourselves again how impossible it would be. You know there's no room for another female in your cousin's house."

Aunt Letty sighed helplessly. "Yes, I know. I keep assuring myself that you'll probably do better here in London than rusticating in Surrey in Hattie's tiny cottage with two old biddies. Here at least you'll have your old room, and all your things about you. . . ."

Miranda smiled ruefully. "Except that china. And my old Aunt."

"Perhaps you should keep the china after all," Aunt Letty suggested suddenly.

"No, I want you to have it. It belongs with you. It was you who brought it to this house when I married."

"As a gift to *you*," the aunt amended.

"Yes, but this house is mine no longer. If it remains here, my sister-in-law will think of it as her own. Belle has plenty of china. She doesn't need this."

"*Can* she claim it as her own?" Letty asked, her bird-like eyes flashing angrily. "Does everything in this house now belong to Charles? Even things you brought with you as a bride?"

Miranda shrugged. "I'm not certain. Mr. Baines said that Charles has ownership of the house and its contents. I didn't ask him about those 'contents' that Mama left to me. But there isn't very much. Just the Sheraton desk. And my bed, of course."

Aunt Letty looked over at the china piled on the floor and frowned. "Then I *will* take the china. I've no wish to add our lovely Minton to the other things Belle Velacott is taking away from you. But you'll have to send the crates to me later on. We shan't have time now to finish the packing."

Reluctantly, they started toward the door, both ladies throwing a last, longing look at the cups, saucers, butter plates and creamed-soup bowls still piled on the floor. "I never should have permitted you to wed him," the older woman suddenly burst out, tears rolling down her wizened cheeks again. "I should have told you what I felt the moment you announced your betrothal."

Miranda stopped and stared at her. "What did you feel?"

"That you were making a terrible mistake. I knew in my bones that Rodney Velacott was an irresponsible rake. I should have warned you. I should have threatened to break with you forever if you went ahead with the wedding. I was a coward."

Miranda almost laughed. "How can you be so silly? I would never have believed so ridiculous a threat. I didn't know much in those days, but I did know that you would stand by me no matter what happened. It was not your cowardice that ruined my life. It was my own vanity. Do you remember, Aunt Letty, what they used to call me?"

"Of course. The Magnificent Miranda."

"Yes, and I was stupid enough to believe them. What a silly young idiot I was. So pleased with myself. So foolishly arrogant. I'd caught the uncatchable Rodney Velacott, and I felt superior to every other girl I knew." She shook her head in bitter amazement at the memory of her younger self. "The Greeks had a word for it, you know. Pride. Hubris. The gods must have had a merry laugh at my expense as they took me down. I suppose I should be thankful they didn't make me blind, like poor King Oedipus."

"You may have been arrogant and foolish," her aunt said as they went up the stairs to collect her things, "but your crime was not so great as to deserve what followed. Why, you had not a single year of happiness with that man."

"No, but I had you to turn to." Miranda threw a tremulous smile at the older woman with heartfelt gratitude. "I thank the Lord for that."

Letty's belongings were already packed. Miranda's abigail and the one remaining housemaid had done the packing this morning, their last household chore before leaving to find other employment. (Miranda had written to Belle and Charles to ask if the maids and Higgins, the groom, could be retained on their household staff: *They have been employed here for years*, she'd written, *and not only are they familiar with the requirements of the house, they are very loyal, honest and deserving employees.* But Belle had written back that she would rather choose her own staff.) Higgins, the last remaining servant in Miranda's employ, would be leaving, too, after he conveyed Letty to her cousin in Surrey and brought back the carriage.

Higgins carried down Letty's things just as the draymen were bringing in the new owners' baggage. The entryway, the passageways and the stairs were scenes of complete confusion. Miranda and Letty could hardly manage a coherent goodbye. To postpone the parting as long as possible, Miranda went out with her aunt to the carriage. There they stood clinging together until Higgins coughed to remind them that the horses should not stand in the cold too long. But even he was tearful at this leave-taking.

Miranda stood there on the windy drive long after Letty's carriage disappeared into the dusk. Then she went in and, ignoring the draymen and the boxes and the disarray of her once-quiet domicile, climbed slowly up to her room, threw herself down on her bed and wept unconsolably. *It isn't fair*, she cried in childish self-pity. *It just isn't fair!*

She knew it was self-pity, but this once she was going to wallow in it. Life had been hellish for the past eleven years, and indeed it *wasn't* fair that her future held no prospects for improvement. How ironic life could be, she thought. She'd started out with such high hopes. She'd won the envy of all her friends when she'd married Rodney, who'd been so handsome, so very well-to-pass, and so determined a bachelor. Winning him had been a triumph for a young woman with no title and very modest means. But her feelings of triumph were short-lived. Within a month of her romantic honeymoon in Italy, after she'd moved into this very house glowing with happiness, she discovered that her new husband had a strong tendency toward drunkenness and lechery.

She'd not wept in those days. Her pride hadn't allowed it. She'd tried other kinds of cajolery: anger, sympathy, warmth, coldness, giving and withholding. But she'd not tried tears. Not at first. But when nothing else seemed to work, she'd even sunk to tears. All to no avail.

And tears are no avail now, she reminded herself, sitting up on her bed. It was all spilt milk. All the tears in the world would not change the past. She dashed them away, got up and went to her dressing table. If her brother-in-law and his wife should appear on the doorstep soon—as seemed likely—she was in no condition to receive them. She took off her apron, brushed the dust from her skirts and turned her attention to her unkempt hair. Hardly glancing at her reflection in the mirror (for her pale, gaunt face gave her little pleasure these days), she gathered her flyaway locks into one long, ropy coil, twisted it into a bun and began to pin it up to the back of her head.

She remembered how Rodney had disliked this way of doing up her hair. He'd always liked it hanging loose. Of course, after the glow of romance had worn thin, he rarely bothered to look at her. By the end of the first year, he was already accusing her of being nagging and burdensome. In fact, the more she indulged in pleas or scolds, the greater was his dislike of the married state. He began to come home at night badly foxed, and sometimes he did not come home at all. Still, she'd found it hard at first to believe that he'd taken a mistress. Later, of course, it was easy to believe. Over the years, he'd kept a succession of them.

She glanced at herself in the mirror. Her hair was neat enough, and her dress—a muslin roundgown with long sleeves and a high neck—was suitable for an evening at home. It had seen better days, but it would have to do. Rodney's brother and his wife would not expect her to greet them in formal attire. But she would make one concession to the occasion and wear her cameo. She took it out of her jewel-box, slipped it on a silver chain and hung it round her neck. It was a lovely piece—a miniature of a lady with a small diamond at her neck. Rodney had bought it for her on their honeymoon. It was not very valuable, Miranda supposed, but it was precious to her. It was her only reminder that she'd once been very, very happy.

But she'd not been at all happy since. Nor did she have any prospects of a change for the better. She wondered, as she stared at the pale, unfamiliar face in the dressing-table mirror, if she should have tried harder to change her life— to leave the man who'd so consistently humiliated her. But what could she have done? She had no parents to run to. Aunt Letty had no home of her own. Miranda had once thought of running off to become an actress on the stage, but it was a childish impulse; she had no talent for such an enterprise. Most women who tried it became, in the end, little better than lightskirts.

All those years, she'd felt quite hopeless. In a society in which divorce was almost unheard of, and where a wife had no rights, there was no way to free herself. Nevertheless, she felt inadequate. She'd failed in the one thing in which a woman was expected to succeed—as a wife. With this awareness of her failure, she had grown more withdrawn. She lost all interest in what had once been her major preoccupation: the pursuit of pleasure. She neither gave nor accepted invitations. She rarely went from home. She withdrew from society in shame.

Was it my fault? she asked her reflection in the mirror. *Was I not charming enough, or beautiful enough, or clever enough?* She knew she'd bored her husband. Her affection bored him. Her disapproval bored him. But then, everything bored him. He was so bored with his life that he could only find relief by gambling. Taking wild risks. Cards, horses or the market, it didn't matter which. All her attempts to reason with him failed. In an attempt to compensate for her husband's wild profligacy, she practiced economy in her home as much as possible, keeping the number of servants to a minimum, ceasing to buy anything but the most necessary items of clothes and household goods, hoarding the household money as best she could. But when, a year ago, her husband was killed—in a final irony, shot in a duel with a man he'd cuckolded—his man of business informed her that there was nothing left of his estate but debts. She had no dower, no jointure, nothing.

She shut her eyes, shuddering at the memory of the day they'd carried him home, everything hushed and secret to prevent the magistrates from learning of the illegal duel. And the poorly-attended funeral during which, numb from shock, she heard not a word of what was said to her. And the reading of the will, in which in the whole of the lengthy document her husband had not made one mention of her name.

She rose from her chair abruptly, for she heard the sounds of carriage wheels on the drive below. They were here! Charles and Belle Velacott had arrived. The moment she'd been dreading for the past year was now upon her. She had to go down, and smile, and make them welcome. There was no time now to dwell on the past.

It was just as well. Remembering the past was too disheartening. But then, contemplating the present was just as disheartening. Once, her hopes for her future had soared as high as the sky. Now reality had brought her down to this: bleak widowhood, impoverishment and the necessity of accepting the charity of Charles and Belle Velacott.

She could hear their voices at the doorway. It was time to go down. She took a deep breath, squared her shoulders and went from her room to face her new life.

How those who knew her before her marriage would laugh if they knew. The Magnificent Miranda, indeed. What a joke!

· Three ·

WITH A SMILE fixed on her face, Miranda reached the last turning on the stairs, but there she paused in surprise. The sight of the confusion in the entry hall below caused her to gasp. The hall was crowded with boxes, crates, pieces of furniture and bulging portmanteaux. Around this mountain of baggage scurried an army of servants that Charles and Belle had brought with them. Miranda counted at least two footmen, four maids, a dignified butler who seemed to be directing traffic, and several other persons whose functions she could not guess. *They must have had to rent a veritable caravan of carriages to transport them all!* Miranda thought.

In the midst of the confusion stood the new owners, Charles and Belle Velacott, happily surveying their new abode. Charles, tall and ruddy-faced, and still wearing his greatcoat (although it hung open to reveal his protuberent midsection), was giving orders to a coachman for the disposition of the horses. Belle, as small in stature as her husband was large, was gazing admiringly at the crystal chandelier over their heads. She was dressed to the nines in a velvet, fur-trimmed pelisse, and, in an apparent attempt to appear taller, carried on her head a high-crowned bonnet with the most enormous plumes Miranda had ever seen. The plumes bobbed about disconcertingly with every motion of the woman's head.

Suddenly Charles caught sight of his sister-in-law on the stairs. "Miranda, my dear," he bellowed, "*there* you are! We are a day early, as you can see. We were too eager to settle in to wait another day."

"Yes, Charles, I quite understand." Miranda ran down the remaining stairs and circled the impedimenta that stood between her and the new arrivals. "Good evening, Belle," she said, bestowing a formal peck on her sister-in-law's cheek. "I hope your trip down from Bedford was pleasant."

"As pleasant as travel with a train of four carriages can be," Belle replied, handing her fur-trimmed pelisse to one of the maids. "I'm glad the journey is over."

"You must be tired. Do go into the sitting room and rest yourselves, while I go and make some tea."

"No need for you to do that any more," Charles said grandly as he shrugged out of his greatcoat. "Our staff is quite ready to work." He signaled to the butler to see to the tea, threw his greatcoat to a footman, and led his wife and his sister-in-law into the sitting room, where one of the maids was already making a fire.

A few moments later, Miranda was enjoying the unusual luxury of being served her tea by a butler and two maids (who had so quickly settled in that they were already in uniform). She began to wonder if her alarm at the prospect of living with the Charles Velacotts had been premature. They were being very cordial. And she had to admit that it was very pleasant to be waited on like this, especially after all those years of caring for this large house almost single-handedly. Perhaps matters were not as desperate as she feared. She sat back in her chair, let the hot drink make its soothing way down her throat, and studied with new eyes the pair with whom she would now be living.

Charles Velacott, Rodney's younger brother and heir, looked older than his thirty-one years, but he had the handsome Velacott profile: aquiline nose, cleft chin and high forehead. Miranda acknowledged that she didn't really dislike him, despite his tendency toward pomposity. Nor did she resent his being Rodney's heir, for his inheritance had added little to his wealth. In truth, he owed his success to no one but himself. He'd gone to the West Indies as a young man and made a small fortune in the molasses trade. This he'd invested wisely, and he was now quite solidly wealthy. All he'd inherited from Rodney were huge debts and some badly-managed family properties which were heavily mortgaged. He'd dealt with the problem by simply selling off the inherited properties—all but this one—to pay the debts.

The Velacott London town house was the one property he'd kept because, as he'd told Miranda later, Belle wanted so much to live here. They would take a year to close up their country home and arrange the move. This, of course, Charles had every right to do. It was not his fault that the house had been Miranda's home for the past eleven years, and that she now had no place to call her own.

Miranda stirred her tea as she threw her brother-in-law a surreptitious glance from under lowered lids. Soothed by the warmth of the fire, the tea and the companionable silence, she was hopeful enough to admit that Charles, though pompous and self-important, was a good-natured, sober fellow, aware of his familial duty, though—and here was the rub!—often prevented by his wife from doing it generously. It was Belle who was the greater problem.

Miranda turned her glance to her sister-in-law, who sat opposite her in a wing chair, still wearing her ridiculous bonnet. The plumes waved every time the woman lifted her cup to her lips. There was no denying that Belle Velacott was a grasping sort who could make even an act of generosity seem vulgar. Miranda's recollection of their conversation after the reading of the will, several months ago, still chilled her blood.

The incident had occurred in this very room. They'd been gathered round the fire just as they were now. It was a few minutes after Mr. Baines, Rodney's solicitor, had departed. Miranda was trying very hard not to weep. "Poor dear Miranda," Charles had murmured, taking her hand in his, "do not add to your grief by believing we do not think of your plight. I quite agree with Mr. Baines that *something* is owed to my brother's widow."

"Though nothing is *legally* required of us," his wife had quickly pointed out.

"But Belle and I have already spoken of this," Charles went on, "and we've decided to offer you a home."

Belle had smiled at her smugly. "A rather generous offer, you must agree."

Miranda, too choked with grief, could not respond.

"A place in our household," Charles had gone on with more than his usual pomp. "A place in our household for the remainder of your lifetime."

"*If* you wish to have it," Belle had added. "You must not feel in the least coerced. And, of course, you do realize that this invitation does not extend to your Aunt Letty. One can only do so much."

Miranda had had to use all her control to keep from flying from the room in tears. The offer could not then—nor did it now—make her feel grateful. In her mind it had seemed rather like a prison sentence. Belle had made it quite plain that she did not really want to share her new home with a sister-in-law she hardly knew. On the few occasions they'd come together since Rodney's death, the woman had been just as she seemed at the reading of the will— smugly condescending. *And that's just how she seems now*, Miranda said to herself as she watched Belle looking about the room with the self-congratulating pride of ownership, her plumes waving.

All these months, the prospect of spending the rest of her life in the same house as Belle Velacott, without even the companionship of her beloved aunt to support her, had been most dismaying to Miranda. But perhaps she'd been wrong. Belle *had* offered her a home, after all. She deserved not to be too hastily judged.

Belle looked up at that moment. "Miranda, my dear, let's not waste time over tea. I do so wish to look over the house. Would you like to show me round?"

"Yes, very much," Miranda said, rising eagerly. "But won't you take off your bonnet first? You are at home now, you know."

They started in the drawing room, where Belle admired the marble mantelpiece and deplored the portrait hanging over it. "What an ugly thing!" she exclaimed. "It must go! I have a fine painting of my mother dandling me on her knee that will be perfect there. Remind me to tell Nash to take care of it, will you?"

They next surveyed the dining room, where Belle's eyes lit up at the sight of the pieces of china still on the floor beside the almost-filled crates. "What lovely china! Minton, isn't it? I shall have to display it in that armoire there."

"I'm sorry, Belle, but you can't," Miranda explained gently. "The china belongs to my aunt. I'm packing it to send out to her."

"Oh, I see," Belle said, disappointment and annoyance very clear in her tone and the set of her chin.

They proceeded through the library (where Belle criticized the placement of the furniture), the music room (where Belle disparaged Miranda's taste in draperies) and the other rooms on the first floor, and then up the stairs. Miranda led Belle straight to the two large, connecting bedrooms that would be hers and Charles's, and the mirrored dressing rooms that adjoined them. To Miranda's relief, Belle seemed quite pleased with their size and furnishings. It was not until Belle noticed a closed door that things went seriously awry. "And what is that?" she asked, pointing.

"That is my room," Miranda said. "Would you care to see it?"

"Of course," Belle responded in a tone that clearly implied, *That room is part of my house, too, isn't it?*

Miranda opened the door and stood aside to let her pass. Belle looked about the room with brows upraised. "Why, it's quite large!" she exclaimed in some surprise.

Miranda suddenly felt guilty, as if she'd somehow overstepped. "Yes, it is," she said defensively, "but not as large as the other two."

"And the windows ... they face south, if I mistake it not."

"Well ... yes, they do."

"I have always favored south-facing rooms," Belle declared sourly. Then her tone changed. "Oh!" she gasped. "*Look* at the *bed*!" She circled the high four-poster, fingering the carvings and eyeing the sheer hangings with a look of pure avarice.

"I believe it's Queen Anne," Miranda offered.

"It *is* Queen Anne," the new mistress of the house declared, her tone clearly accusing Miranda of stealing the best of the furnishings for herself.

"It was my mother's," Miranda said quietly. "It is one of the few things of value that I brought with me when I was wed."

"Oh, I see," Belle murmured, taken aback. She bit her lip, resentful and annoyed to learn that she was not mistress of *everything* in this house. "It seems a very fine piece."

"Thank you." Miranda wondered if she was expected to apologize for reserving for herself something of value. But she swallowed her irritation and tried to recapture the good feelings with which she'd started out on this tour. "Would you care to see the other rooms on this floor?" she asked pleasantly. "There's a little room down the hall that might do very well as a writing room for you. It has a lovely old desk inset with porcelain tiles, a Sheraton. I'm sure the room will please you—the windows also face south."

The desk, a large, eight-legged, ornate piece with solid gold pulls and magnificently-painted tiles, made a very distinct impression on Belle. "I suppose you'll now tell me," she said sarcastically as she ran her fingers over the polished surface, "that this was your mother's, too."

"I wasn't going to," Miranda retorted, stung by Belle's tone, "but as a matter of fact it was."

From Belle's snort, Miranda knew that the grasping little woman did not believe her. They proceeded on, but the feeling of warmth with which Miranda had begun the expedition was gone forever.

After the house had been thoroughly examined, and an impromptu buffet supper had been served in the dining room, Miranda excused herself and bid her new hosts good night. She needed to be alone to think over the day's events. She was still willing to try to find something about Belle to like, but the prospects were gloomy.

Half an hour later, she heard a tap on her door. Already in her nightdress, she only opened it a crack. In the corridor stood Nash, the butler. "I beg pardon for disturbing you at this hour, ma'am," he said, "but Mr. Velacott would like a word with you in the library before you retire."

"But I've already retired," she objected.

The butler bit his lip. "I believe," he said uncomfortably, "that Mr. Velacott feels that this matter shouldn't wait till morning."

"Very well. Tell him I'll be down as soon as I can dress."

In the library, Miranda found Charles pacing back and forth before the fire, looking very unhappy. His wife was nowhere in evidence. "Do sit down, my dear," he began, not ceasing his pacing. "I don't quite know how to tell you this."

"Just say it outright, whatever it is," Miranda said, sitting down at the edge of an armchair facing him. "I dislike roundaboutation."

"Well, then, without roundaboutation, here it is. My wife feels . . . that is, we *both*—she wants me to make it clear that I speak for both of us—*we* feel that your room is . . . well, it faces south, you see, and our bedrooms face west. Belle does love . . . that is, we *both* like a south-facing room . . ." His voice failed him, and he flicked her a look of sheer misery.

Miranda tried to make sense of this meandering speech. "Are you saying that Belle wants me to exchange my bedroom for hers?" she asked in disbelief. "But she can't be serious. In the first place, hers is much larger. And in the second, it adjoins yours. I can't take a bedroom adjoining yours."

"No, no, of course not. I did not explain properly." He took another quick turn across the room. "Damnation," he muttered to himself, "Belle should be doing this herself." He threw Miranda another shamefaced glance. "But she was very tired. It has been a long day."

"Yes, it certainly has. But you were saying . . . ?"

"Yes, about your room. She . . . we . . . are quite content with our bedrooms. We don't want your room as a bedroom but as a . . . a sitting room for Belle. Facing south, you see."

"A sitting room. Facing south. I see." Miranda swallowed hard. "And where would Belle . . . and you, of course . . . like me to sleep?"

"She says there's another south-facing room down the hall that would be very pleasant for you. She says you'll know which one she means. You thought it might be a nice writing room for her."

"Yes, I know the one. But, Charles, it is very small. I don't believe there's a wall wide enough to accommodate my bed."

"Belle's thought of that. She says that her bed is a good deal smaller than yours. She said to tell you she'd be willing to exchange her bed for yours."

"Would she, indeed?" Miranda rose from her chair. Her knees were trembling. "How very kind of her," she said between stiff lips. "Does she wish to make the exchange tonight, or may I sleep in my own bed for one more night?"

Charles's eyes dropped from her face. "Certainly you may stay where you are tonight," he muttered awkwardly. He turned to the fire and lowered his head till his forehead rested on the mantel. "Tomorrow will be soon enough to move things about."

"Then I bid you another good night, sir." And she strode quickly to the door.

"Miranda, I . . ." He looked up over his shoulder at her, his eyes more miserable than before. "I'm truly sorry. But there is one more thing. In your new room, Belle noticed—"

"I know. You don't have to say it. She wants the desk."

He reddened to the ears. "Well, you *will* have a bit more room without it."

"So I will," Miranda agreed, adding as she pulled the door closed behind her, "How considerate of Belle to think of that."

She was trembling with fury by the time she reached her room. *That blasted female!* she cursed in her mind. *She has everything in the world! Must she have my bed, too?*

She could not sleep. She prowled about her room for hours, like a tiger caged. In one short evening, Belle had proved herself selfish and manipulating. There was no other way to describe her. Was it to be Miranda's fate to spend the rest of her life in the same house with such a woman?

No! she told herself vehemently. There *had* to be another way she could live. She had to find a way to support herself, there was no other choice. She had to find work of some kind. Anything, any kind of humble life, would be better than to be in this humiliating, degrading position. She would be a barmaid in a tavern, a lady's maid, a cook . . . anything! There was work to be had in this world. Hadn't she seen, this very afternoon, a list of advertisements—?

She gasped, blinking into the darkness, as an idea took hold. Quickly she lit a candle, slipped out of her room and ran down the stairs to the dining room. Shaking with eagerness, she set the candle on the floor, knelt before the still-open packing crate and took out the last saucer she'd wrapped. She unwrapped it and spread the crumpled newspaper on the floor. According to the date at the top of the page, it was almost a month old, but she prayed she would not be too late. In the dim candlelight, she skimmed the column of advertisements. There it was, just as she remembered it: *Mrs. Terence Traherne of Wymondham, Norfolk, seeks the assistance of a gentlewoman to supervise the education of three boys, ages five through twelve.* She had never supervised the education of anyone, but she *was* a gentlewoman. Perhaps she might qualify!

She ripped the advertisement from the page and dashed back up the stairs to the room into which she was to be moved at daybreak. She set her candlestick on the Sheraton desk that Belle lusted after and propped the torn piece of paper up against it. Then she pulled a sheet of writing paper and a quill from a drawer, cut a point, dipped it in an inkwell and began to write: *To Mrs. Terence Traherne of Norfolk: Dear Madam, In response to your advertisement in the London Times of 15 October* . . .

· Four ·

THE HONORABLE BARNABY Traherne turned up the collar of his greatcoat and huddled deeper into the cushions of the stagecoach seat. *December,* he said to himself, shivering, *is not the time to travel north.* The wind rattled the loose-fitting windows and whistled in at the edges of the doors, making the inside of the carriage feel as cold as outdoors. He'd had to rise before five this morning, dress in the dark and hurry through the cold streets to the Swan With Two Necks Inn to catch the stage. *Perhaps I shouldn't have agreed to go to Terence's for Christmas,* he mused. *I could still have been comfortably asleep right now, and I could have spent the holidays lazing about in my flat right here in London.*

He glanced over at the one other passenger, a heavyset fellow with a florid complexion and a bulbous nose, who was busily chewing away on a large sugared bun and seemed undisturbed by the cold. At first Barnaby, who hated any sort of crush, had been glad there were no other passengers on the London-to-Norwich stage, but now he was sorry; two more passengers on each of the wide seats would have made the coach warmer. But there was still a stop to be made at Islington before the coach turned onto the North Road. Undoubtedly, a few more passengers would be picked up there.

He opened the newspaper he'd purchased at the Swan before departure but then resisted the compulsion to read it. He was on holiday, after all. He didn't want to trouble his mind with his usual foreign-office concerns: the unrest in Germany, Turkey's troubles with the Serbs, the workers' riots in Derbyshire, and all the rest. The world, in spite of its problems, would surely keep on turning on its axis without him.

He turned to the window and gazed out at the passing landscape, but it gave little pleasure. The sky hung heavy and dark over a gray December world, and to make things worse, a few flakes of snow drifted by his window. Snow! That was all he needed to solidify his regrets that he'd undertaken this journey. It would be seven o'clock at night—eleven hours from now—when the stage would reach Barnaby's destination, Wymondham. There he expected to be met by his brother's carriage, which would take him three miles west, probably another half hour of travel. It would be a long, tedious day before he reached his destination. If a heavy snowfall should develop, and the coach delayed, it would be the last straw!

To Barnaby's relief, the sprinkle of snowflakes dissipated by the time the coach pulled in to the innyard of the Queen's Head at Islington. The sonorous chimes of the bells in St. Mary's Church were ringing out the hour of eight. The yard of the Queen's Head was usually alive with activity at this hour, with ostlers and stableboys and porters dashing in and out among the waiting passengers. But this morning, Barnaby was surprised to see only one passenger waiting to board. The freezing weather had undoubtedly deterred most of the travelers. The lone passenger, a woman, was being cruelly battered by the wind. With her pelisse whipping about her and her skirts billowing, she had to hold on to her bonnet with one gloved hand while directing a porter where to stow her two large portmanteaux with the other.

Barnaby, having turned his attention to his newspaper, barely glanced at the woman as she climbed into the carriage and brushed by his knees to take a seat opposite him. But the other passenger lifted his hat. "Good morning, ma'am," he said in so obsequious a tone that Barnaby assumed the woman must be pretty, "Augustus Woodley, at your service."

Barnaby glanced over the top of his newspaper to see if his surmise was correct, but the woman was turned away from him, for she was nodding politely to Mr. Woodley in acknowledgement of his greeting. When she turned back, he got a glimpse of her face. At the sight of it, he felt a sharp tightening of his stomach even before his brain registered her identity. *Good God*, he thought, horrified, *it can't be! Not . . . Miranda Pardew!*

Instinctively, he hid himself behind his newspaper. He must be mistaken, he told himself. Miranda Pardew, or whatever her name was now, would not be taking a journey on a public conveyance, without a maid or companion. She could not travel like any ordinary housewife. Besides, his impression of this woman, quick as it was, was of a rather dowdy person of middle age. She seemed to be dressed somberly, her pelisse more serviceable than decorative and her gown a subdued grayish blue. As for her bonnet, it was not at all the high-crowned sort that women of fashion liked to wear. *No, no*, he assured himself, *it can't possibly be she*.

Slowly, he lowered the newspaper and squinted over it. Fortunately, the woman was engaged in searching through her reticule for something, enabling him to take a long look at her. Though not middle-aged, she was certainly past the flush of youth. Her skin was very pale, her eyes (which he had to admit were still beautiful, tilted upward in the corners and thickly fringed with dark lashes) seemed red-rimmed as if she'd been weeping, her lips were tightly pressed together, and her hair so primly pulled back from her face that it was completely hidden by her bonnet. One *might* call that face lovely, he admitted reluctantly, but it was no longer a face that would attract the eyes of half the men in a ballroom. Yet it *was* Miranda Pardew. There was no mistaking her.

As she fished a handkerchief from her reticule, he quickly ducked behind his paper. The act filled him with shame. What was he afraid of? It was unlikely that she would

recognize him. They had met only once, and although
she'd left an indelible mark on *him*, he had certainly not
left a mark on *her*.

Nevertheless, he kept his eyes fixed on his newspaper
for the next hour or so. During that time, Mr. Woodley
tried repeatedly to engage the lady in conversation, but he
received only murmured monosyllables for his pains. When
they stopped at Epping to change horses and take a bite of
luncheon, Barnaby watched Woodley follow the lady into
the inn. She obviously tried to avoid him, but the fellow
was persistent. Later, when Barnaby entered the taproom,
he saw that Woodley had seated himself beside the lady at
her table. Barnaby took a table near the window where he
would not be in her direct line of vision but where he could
observe them. As he ate his bread and ham and sipped at his
mulled ale, he saw that Woodley's attentions were bringing
a look of chagrin to the lady's face. Barnaby wondered why
she didn't give the fellow a set-down. She'd certainly been
very good at that in her youth. Had she lost the knack?

When they returned to the carriage, Miss Pardew (or
whatever her name now was), the first to climb aboard,
took a seat on the opposite side. It was a clear message to
Mr. Woodley that she wished to avoid him, but he did not
take the hint. Shoving himself up the coach steps ahead
of Barnaby, he plopped down beside her, in the seat that
Barnaby had occupied earlier. When Barnaby seated himself on the other side, the lady threw him a helpless glance,
as if she were pleading with him to change seats. Nothing
in that glance, however, showed even the tiniest bit of rec-
ognition. He looked back at her coldly and lifted his paper
up between them. *If you need help ma'am,* he told her in his
mind, *I'm the last man in the world who'll offer it to you.*

He knew he was not being gentlemanly, but she deserved
no politeness from him. Miss Miranda Pardew was repug-
nant to him. When he was nineteen she'd treated him with
merciless contempt, and even if she was now past her bloom
and looking dowdy and plain, he didn't care. He remembered reading somewhere that one might forgive injuries but

no one ever forgave contempt. How true. How very true.

He turned to the window and noticed, to his chagrin, that the snow had begun to fall again. And if this were not enough to raise his ire, he had to listen to Augustus Woodley's revolting attempts to gain the interest of Miss Pardew. The fellow kept up a barrage of asinine comments which did nothing to endear him to the woman he was trying to impress. "My, but you have tiny feet," he'd remark. Or, "Those are very fine-looking gloves. What do you call their color?"

These ploys were greeted with only a stony silence.

"It's getting a lot colder, ma'am," Woodley remarked several times. "Let me give you my muffler." Once he actually tried to wind it about her neck. She had to fend him off.

Barnaby tried not to pay attention to the goings-on. But the lady's restraint surprised him. The girl he'd met at the ball would certainly not have kept her sharp tongue in check. She'd known quite well, back then, how to put a man in his place. Indeed, she seemed much changed in many ways. The slate-blue Kerseymere gown she was now wearing, with its prim white collar, straight skirt and simple gimp-cord trim, was a far cry from the clinging, enticing, soft green silk she'd worn the night of the ball. And her bonnet sported no feathers or ornamentation—it was modest in height and brim and was tied under her chin with the plainest of bows. She neither looked, dressed nor behaved like a belle of the *ton*. He couldn't help wondering if, perhaps, some sort of tragedy had befallen her.

While he was thus studying her, he noticed that the obnoxiously persistent Augustus Woodley had moved his leg to rest against Miss Pardew's thigh. The lady edged away. A few moments later, Mr. Woodley moved again. Miss Pardew edged away again. When the dunderpate moved a third time, and the lady, wedged tightly between him and the armrest, had no place to move, Barnaby had had enough. With an exclamation of disgust, he tossed his newspaper down, jumped to his feet and grabbed the fellow by the collar of his coat. "You don't seem comfortable, Woodley," he said, lifting the fellow bodily and throwing him over to the opposite seat. "I think you'll be happier sitting beside *me*." And he re-seated himself, picked up the newspaper and opened it to his place.

"Oh, I *say*!" Woodley cried in outrage when he regained his breath. "What do you think you're about?"

"I know what I'm about. And I know what you're about. So take my advice, fellow. Stay put and hold your tongue. We've had enough of your buffoonery."

Woodley opened his mouth to retort, caught a glimpse of Barnaby's glower that had intimidated so many others, reddened and retreated to his corner.

The lady threw Barnaby a look of melting gratitude. "Thank you, sir," she said softly, the corners of her lips turning up in a suggestion of a smile.

Barnaby did not smile back. He merely fixed his glower on her and, with cold deliberation, lifted up the newspaper between them. He could deliver a set-down, too.

How the lady took his set-down he didn't know, for he kept his eyes fixed on his newspaper. The journey proceeded in absolute silence. The only sounds were those of the carriage wheels, the horses' hooves and the whistling wind.

That was why, later that afternoon, on a deserted stretch of road between Barton Mills and Thetford, they all heard the clip-clop of other horses rapidly coming up from behind them. These sounds were followed by shouts, and the carriage rocked to an abrupt stop. Before they had time to interpret these signs, the door near Woodley was pulled open, and they found themselves staring into the black barrel of an ominously long pistol. Mr. Woodley started. The lady gasped. Barnaby let his newspaper drift to the floor.

A head appeared in the doorway, the eyes covered with a black mask. "Hands over yer heads, gents! And the lady, too. Quick now!" The voice had a low, frightening rasp.

All three did as they were told, but Barnaby was more irritated than frightened. "A damned *highwayman*!" he exclaimed in disgust. "Just what I needed."

· Five ·

THEY STEPPED DOWN from the carriage into an icy wind and a swirl of light snowflakes. The masked footpad, a large, broadly built fellow as tall as Barnaby, looked from one to the other and chose Mr. Woodley to fleece first. Without a word, and keeping one eye and the barrel of his gun aimed at the other two, he efficiently set about removing Mr. Woodley's valuables: his watch, chain and fobs, and his purse.

Barnaby used the time to look about. They were standing in a rutted roadway edged on both sides by woodland. There was no sign of human habitation. He noted that the highwayman was not alone, for two horses were tethered to a nearby tree. A quick glance toward the front of the coach revealed a second felon, also masked, but much shorter and slighter than his confederate. He was aiming a pistol at the coachman, who was hesitating to climb down from the box. "Move yer arse down 'ere," the footpad ordered. "I don't 'ave all day."

The coachman's arm made a swift movement downward. Barnaby saw his hand grasp the trace of the horse on the left and break it loose, thus unhooking the harness. Before the footpad realized what he was up to, the coachman had leaped to the horse's back, dug his heels into the horse's side and was galloping off, the harness dragging behind him. The horse on the right whinnied wildly, reared up, broke from his already-loosened trace and quickly followed. The footpad cursed, aimed his gun and fired, but the rider and both horses were already disappearing into the distance. The whole incident had taken but a few seconds.

The second highwayman cursed again, very loudly. The stir had drawn the eyes of the others, who were grouped at the side of the carriage. "Damn you, Japhet," the first highwayman shouted. "Whyn't ye watch—?"

But he got no further, for Barnaby had taken immediate advantage of his distraction and leaped forward, grasping the arm holding the gun. The tall highwayman dropped the gun, but not before a shot exploded into the air, causing the lady to scream. Barnaby and the highwayman toppled to the ground, rolling back and forth, first one on top and then the other. Barnaby was getting the better of the fight when the second highwayman, having reloaded, ran over and aimed his pistol at Barnaby's head. "Let 'im go or ye're a dead man," he said coldly.

Barnaby let go. Both men got to their feet. The highwayman retrieved his pistol and turned to his cohort. "It's all yer fault, ye blasted looby," he snarled as he reloaded. "Ye couldn' even 'andle the coachman."

"You ain't doin' so bloody well yerself," the one named Japhet retorted. "Seems t' me like you also lost one."

It was quite true. One of the three passengers was gone. During the melee, Augustus Woodley had managed to steal off. "Howsomever, old chubb," the taller footpad bragged, "I nimmed 'is goods afore 'e ran." And he waved Woodley's watch in the other fellow's face.

"Damn it, woman," Barnaby muttered to the lady, "you should have gone off with your admirer."

Miranda threw Barnaby a startled look and opened her mouth to make a reply, but before she could do so, the tall highwayman swung round to Barnaby. "Still yer clapper!" he snapped. "Not one word or one move more, or it'll be the worser fer ye. Keep yer weapon on 'im, Japhet, while I go through 'is pockets."

Barnaby's pockets produced the best of the loot. The highwayman gurgled with pleasure at the purse he found, heavy with guineas. And when he saw Barnaby's watch, gleaming with heavy gold and attached to a chain that bore a beautiful, jewel-studded fob (a gift from the Earl on the occasion of Barnaby's thirtieth birthday), he turned to Japhet with a shout of triumph. "Will ye clamp yer peepers on *this*?" he chortled.

Barnaby, cold, furious and humiliated, could bear no more. Grasping the fellow by the back of his collar, he pulled him around and landed him a facer on the side of his jaw. The miscreant staggered back, dizzied. Barnaby struck the fellow's arm a smart blow that sent the watch and chain flying from his hand. At the same moment, he made a lunge for the pistol. But the second felon, Japhet, shook himself into action and swung the butt of his pistol at Barnaby's head. Barnaby fell down, stunned.

He tried to lift his head, but the motion made the world spin round at so terrifying a speed he had to close his eyes. He dropped his head with a groan. When he opened his eyes again, he was staring into the barrel of Japhet's pistol. Off to the side the other footpad was digging about among the dead leaves and foliage at the edge of the road, evidently searching for the watch that Barnaby had made him drop. "Put the bullet in 'is noddle an' be done," he was saying, "so you can come over 'ere and 'elp me search."

Japhet cocked the pistol and aimed. Barnaby tensed. With a cry, the lady leaped upon the felon and knocked his arm aside. Though the report made Barnaby wince and the lady shriek, the bullet flew harmlessly into the air. The other footpad did not even look round. "I found it," he cried happily, holding up the watch.

Japhet, enraged by the woman's interference, pulled Miranda to her feet and lifted his hand to strike her across the face. She lifted her chin arrogantly. "Murderer!" she snapped. "Will you also strike a defenseless woman?"

"Finish 'em off, both of 'em," the tall highwayman instructed. "Then we won't 'ave to watch 'em whiles we go through the baggage."

"That would be a stupid thing to do," Barnaby said with deliberate nonchalance. It was a tone he'd learned to use in handling difficult negotiations in the foreign service.

"Stupid, eh? Ha! So you say," the tall highwayman sneered. "I'd say it too in yer place."

But Japhet, the other one, was caught by Barnaby's tone. "Why stupid?" he asked, his interest caught.

"The coachman managed to hold on to his horses, isn't that so?" Barnaby reasoned. "Sooner or later he'll return for his carriage. With his coach and his horses intact, he will have lost nothing belonging to him or to his employer. He'll probably be content to return to London without further ado. But if he finds two bodies lying here, he will certainly feel compelled to go for the magistrates."

The tall highwayman was not impressed. "So we'll bury yer bodies."

"In this frozen ground? It'll take hours."

" 'E's right," Japhet said, looking at his partner worriedly. "That coachy's a rum cove. 'E mought be back any time soon."

The tall footpad considered the situation for a moment. "Then just tie 'em up to that tree," he said at last, starting toward the back of the coach where the baggage was tied. "An' be certain sure that the tongue-paddler's hands is tied tight."

Japhet marched his prisoners to the tree indicated. Keeping a sharp eye on them, he backed over to his horse and removed a length of rope from a saddlebag. He made the lady tie Barnaby's hands behind him and then bound them both to the tree. After checking that all knots were tight, he went to help his cohort rifle through the baggage.

"That was a clever argument you used to save our lives," Miranda said to the man tied beside her. "You must indeed be a tongue-paddler."

"I can't say, ma'am," Barnaby answered coldly, "since I have no idea what a tongue-paddler is."

"It's a thief's word for lawyer."

"A thief's word, eh? I don't find it particularly reassuring to know that the woman to whom I'm tied is familiar with thieves' cant."

The lady gave a gurgling laugh. "I don't see why it should worry you. Even if I were a thief, you've nothing to fear. They've already taken all your valuables."

He glared at her over his shoulder. "I'm delighted that my losses provide you with a subject for amusement, ma'am. When you find yourself slowly freezing to death, I hope you're able to laugh at that."

"Freezing to death? But you said the coachman would be back soon."

"I said it to keep those felons from blowing out our brains. It's much more likely that the coachman is halfway back to London by this time. With the snow getting heavier, I'm certain he'll want to be back before it accumulates."

"Oh, dear," Miranda said worriedly, "I never thought—"

But she ceased speaking, for the two miscreants were coming toward them, their arms laden with loot. Japhet carried a load of assorted clothing, while his confederate lugged a wooden crate from which the top had been pried off. Inside were more than a dozen bottles of what Barnaby believed was Scotch whiskey. The thieves had got themselves a good haul.

The tall highwayman, who wanted to be certain he could not possibly be followed, approached his prisoners to make a last check on their bonds. It was then he discovered he'd overlooked something. "Well, well," he chortled, " 'ere's a rum bit I almost missed. The lady still 'as 'er reticule."

Japhet clucked his tongue. "Tch, tch, ol' chum. Gettin' a mite careless, eh? What else mought the lady 'ave on 'er person?"

"Let's see." He pulled off Miranda's gloves and examined her wrists and fingers. He made her remove her wedding ring. (*So she* is *wed*, Barnaby noted.) Then he removed her bonnet and the lace cap she wore under it, causing her hair to tumble down over her shoulders, but no clips or jewels were revealed among the auburn tresses. He finally pulled open her pelisse at the neck with so rough a jerk that he ripped out the hook. "Nothin' much else," he muttered, disappointed. "Just this pretty bauble hangin' round 'er neck." And he yanked her cameo from its chain.

"Please don't take that," Miranda pleaded. "Please. It isn't very valuable, but it's very dear to me."

"That's whut they all say," the highwayman sneered, looking over the piece appreciatively.

"I didn't say it about my watch," Barnaby pointed out.

"Wouldn't do ye much good if ye did. I knowed the minute I seed it that it was a fancy timepiece. I wouldn' take a cent less than twenny quid fer it from my fence."

"Only twenty guineas?" Barnaby snorted disparagingly. "You'd be a fool."

The highwayman peered at Barnaby intently with a gleam so calculating that it was apparent even behind his mask. " 'Ow much would it take fer me *not* to be a fool?" he asked.

"Give the lady back her bauble, and I'll tell you exactly what it's worth."

"Not a chance." He pocketed the cameo and walked toward his horse. "I'll ask the fence fer fifty quid, then. That'll be a good enough price fer me."

The two miscreants tied their loot on their horses' backs, jumped up into the saddles and rode off without a backward look. Soon the sound of their horses' hooves was swallowed up by the wind.

Barnaby stared straight ahead of him at the swirling snow, the flakes growing thicker and coming down heavier every minute, and silently cursed his fate. He could imagine nothing worse than being out in this freezing weather tied helplessly to a tree beside the last woman in the world he would have chosen for company.

A slight movement—the tiniest tremor—from the woman beside him made him turn his head in her direction. Flakes of snow were accumulating on her bare head. Her thick auburn hair was tumbled about her shoulders, hiding her face from his view. "I say," he asked, surprised, "are you crying?"

"No, no, of c-course not," she retorted in a choked voice. "Why should I be c-crying? I'm tied to a tree with a man who thought I should have run off with a lecherous toad, it's snowing, I'm likely to freeze to death in my bonds, my portmanteaux have been rifled and my clothes are lying tossed about on the ground, all my money has been taken from me, and I've even l-lost my l-lovely c-c-cameo. What on earth is there to c-cry about?"

"Crying is wasted effort," Barnaby responded calmly. "We should be using our energies to cut ourselves loose."

She drew in a trembling breath. "I would be happy to use my energies in that way. What do you suggest I do?"

"Try to wriggle closer to me. The less room we take, the looser the bonds. If we can loosen these ropes enough to allow you to move your hands, you might be able to reach into my coat pocket there on my right. There's a pocket knife in it."

"A knife?" Her voice took on a glimmer of hope. She began to inch closer to him. "How is it possible the knife escaped the notice of those thieves?"

"Carelessness. I think the tall fellow was so overjoyed at the weight of my purse that he looked no further."

She was quite close to him now. He could feel her pressing against his side. Her arm twisted against the ropes, giving her just enough slack to permit her hand to inch slowly up his leg to his coat pocket. The effort made her breathe heavily. "I can feel the opening," she said, "but I can't reach in. Can you lower yourself a bit?"

He managed to do so, but the ropes cut into his chest painfully. Her hand was in his pocket now, feeling about for the little knife. "Hurry, can't you?" he gasped. "I can't keep bent like this much longer."

"I'm doing the very best . . . There! I have it!"

But that was only the first step. The next problem was to pull out the knife's intricately-imbedded blade, a trick that required two hands. "You'll have to try to bring your other hand over," he told her.

The effort caused so much friction against the ropes that her wrist was rubbed raw. By the time she managed to open the little knife, it was getting dark. She sawed the rope closest to her hand with the little blade, but it was slow work.

While she labored, Barnaby had time to examine her face at close range. His earlier assessment of her appearance had been hasty, he decided. She was still quite lovely. Snowflakes glistened on her cheeks, emphasizing the translucence of her skin; they caught on her long lashes and bejeweled her marvelous, thick, red-tinged hair. And her throat! How well he remembered that voluptuously shapely throat. It was her throat that had first caught his eye all those years ago. And it was still the same. She was not so changed as he had first thought.

Her closeness stirred his blood. He could feel her breast pressed against his arm and her thigh against his leg. And her breath, warm and sweet-smelling, blew against his neck as she labored. It was enough to make any man weak in the knees. If only she were someone else . . . *anyone* else but Miranda Pardew. He could not let himself forget who she was, and what she'd done to him.

Once the first piece of rope was cut through, the rest went quickly. She unbound them from the tree and then set to work on the bonds that tied his wrists. "That took long enough," he said ungraciously when he was at last freed.

She threw him a look of astonishment. "What a very sullen fellow you are, to be sure," she remarked. "But I suppose I should understand. You've lost more even than I."

"You needn't make excuses for me, ma'am," he retorted, rubbing his wrists. "I am sullen by nature. But we have no time for bibble-babble. It's getting dark, I'm already chilled to the bone, as you too must be, and we have at least three miles to walk."

"To where, may I ask?"

"To a small inn we passed back there, a few moments before those footpads stopped us."

"You are admirably observant, sir," she said, "but shouldn't we rather go forward, in the direction in which we were headed?"

"No, for who knows how far we'd have to walk to find habitation. It's better to go toward certainty than doubt."

"Yes, I suppose you're right," she agreed. "Just give me a few moments to gather up what's left of my things."

"I won't give you a few moments. In the first place, it's growing too dark. In a little while, we won't even see the road. In the second place, I have no intention of lugging a portmanteau three miles through the snow."

She stiffened in offense. "I had no intention of asking you. I'll 'lug' it myself."

He grasped her cruelly by the arm and turned her toward the road. "No, you will not. You'll need all your strength and breath to manage the three miles—and it may be more, for all I know—in this wind and cold. Perhaps someone at the inn can be coerced into coming back for your things. Move along now, like a good girl."

She shook off his hold angrily. "May I at least have a moment to retrieve my bonnet?"

His answer was an impatient grunt. She picked up the mistreated headpiece from the ground where the highwayman had dropped it, brushed off the snow and set it on her head. Then she hurried down the road after him, rubbing her arm where he'd grasped it. "Sullen is too kind an adjective to describe you," she snapped as she caught up with him and fell into step beside him. "I've never before met such a rudesby as you. One would think that, sometime in the past, somewhere, somehow, I had done you an injury."

He did not bother to respond.

· Six ·

THEY HAD TO walk more than five miles, Barnaby esti-
mated, before they saw the lights of the inn flickering
through the snowflakes. It felt like twenty-five miles. His
feet were damp and icy-cold, his fingers frozen and his
ears numb. And the woman beside him was in an even
worse case. Her nose was red, her teeth chattered and
there were frozen tears on her cheeks, tears more likely
to have been brought on by the assault of the icy wind
than by self-pity. She was a game chit, he had to grant
her that, for she never made a word of complaint. He was
certain that her feet were colder than his, for she wore
only little leather half-boots—like a man's high-lows—
which were too short and too flimsy to protect against
the rapidly deepening snow. Despite his old, unchanging
dislike of her, he was unable to keep from feeling pity for
her plight. He could not supply her with protection for her
feet, but he'd twice offered to give her his greatcoat. Each
time she'd waved him off. "I will not be beholden to such a
rudesby," she'd said dismissively. And those were the only
words they exchanged during the long, cold march.

The lights of the inn made a welcome gleam in the
darkness, and when the travelers slogged into the courtyard, the actual sight of it was truly comforting. The inn
looked warm and inviting. Its snow-spattered sign, lit by

the guttering flame of a brass lantern and creaking as it swung in the wind, read *Deacon's Gate Inn*. It was small for a public house, with two picturesque bow windows and a thickly-thatched roof, quite like a cottage in a Mother Goose picture book. But the most welcome sight of all was the smoke billowing from the two chimneys at each side of the house; evidently there were some goodly fires burning within.

Barnaby pushed open the door and followed Miranda into the blessed warmth. As they stamped the snow from their shoes in the tiny vestibule, a middle-aged woman (with a head of wild, though faded, red hair pinned so carelessly atop her head that much of it was falling about her face) appeared in the doorway of what was probably a taproom. "Bless me sainted mither!" she exclaimed in a thick brogue. "What wind o' the de'il blew ye here in this storm?"

"Only shank's mare," Barnaby said shortly. "For God's sake, woman, save your questions and take the lady to a fire."

"Aye, sir. Yer lady does look frozen through." The woman promptly put a proprietary arm about Miranda's waist and led her into the taproom, a room only large enough to accommodate three tables. But the fireplace was huge, and an appropriately large fire crackled within it. Miranda knelt before the blaze and, pulling off her thin gloves, held her hands up to the warmth.

The woman studied the kneeling Miranda with a look of sympathy before removing her soaked bonnet and pelisse. Then she turned to another door in the far corner. "Hanlon, ye lazy sot, come out 'ere," she shouted. " 'Tis company we 'ave! They'll be wantin' a hot toddy, so shake yer leg, me man!"

A moment later, a man appeared carrying two mugs. Short and bald, his florid face exuded good humor. He greeted the lady at the fireplace and handed her a tankard. " 'Tis a specialty of the 'ouse," he explained, smiling broadly, "called a Lamb's Wool. The name's a mite unfittin', but it'll warm yer innards."

Miranda accepted the drink gratefully and took a swig at once. The innkeeper, meanwhile, crossed the room to Barnaby. " 'Ere, sir, let me 'ave that wet coat o' yourn. Just drink this down, an' you'll be feelin' better afore it's gone."

"A Lamb's Wool, eh?" Barnaby sniffed into the tankard suspiciously. "What's in it?"

"Cider an' home brew an' a bit o' the grape," the innkeeper said as he went off with the wet outergarments. "Nothin' at all t' trouble yer stomach."

Barnaby drank a draught and discovered that the innkeeper had the right of it. A delicious warmth spread through his body. Never had he tasted so satisfying a brew.

The innkeeper's wife came up to him and watched with a pleased grin as he drank. "Good, ain't it? No one's ever had a bad word fer my husband's Lamb's Wool. And now you'll be wantin' a hot supper, I'll be bound."

"Yes, indeed, Mrs. Hanlon—it is Mrs. Hanlon, is it not?— some supper will be most welcome. Anything you have on hand, so long as it's hot. And afterwards, of course, a place to sleep for the night."

"That goes wi'out sayin'. 'Tain't a night fer man 'r beast out there."

Barnaby, looking down at the woman's friendly, guile-less face, felt dishonest for accepting her hospitality without telling her he could not pay for it. He decided that the only honorable thing to do was to be frank with her. Not wishing to involve Miranda in sordid money matters, he motioned to Mrs. Hanlon to follow him into the vestibule. "Before we proceed any further, Mrs. Hanlon," he confided in a low voice, "I think I'd better tell you that the Norfolk stage on which we were traveling was beset by highwaymen. We were robbed of every valuable we possessed. Thus, I've not a groat on my person with which to pay you. I won't be able to settle the bill until I pass this way again after the New Year. Do you think you can trust me until then?"

"Ha!" came a snort from behind him. Barnaby looked round to find the hitherto-beaming innkeeper standing in the doorway, but he now had no smile on his face. "*Trust* ye?" he exclaimed contemptuously. "Don't take us fer fools. We been ast fer trust afore. You ain't the first what claimed that highwaymen emptied yer pockets. But that don't mean I'll let ye try to empty ours!"

Barnaby was not accustomed to having his word doubted, but his diplomatic training had taught him that one doesn't win an argument by losing one's temper. "You do believe we were robbed, don't you? You can go to see the abandoned coach for yourself when the snow lets up," he pointed out reasonably. "It's only five miles up the road."

"Oh, we 'ave no doubt ye was robbed," Mrs. Hanlon said, throwing a glare at her husband. "That stretch o' road up north is a footpad's dream."

"Then you've dealt with their victims before?"

"And been cheated by 'em, too, givin' them trust," the innkeeper said scornfully. "At least the footpads, when they come," he added under his breath, "pay fer their shot in cash."

Barnaby did not miss the implications of that muttered remark. The innkeeper had had dealings with the footpads in the past. That was useful information for the future, when he returned to deal with the felons.

Meanwhile, the redheaded Mrs. Hanlon wheeled on her husband. "Hanlon, still yer clapper, and don' be a looby! Can't ye see that this here's a gen'leman? One look should tell ye 'e's the sort'll keep 'is word. An' there's naught to be done in any case. We can't put 'em out in the snow, now, can we?"

The innkeeper frowned, shook his head and stomped back to where he'd come from, muttering something about women being as suited to business as cats to water.

Mrs. Hanlon was not in the least perturbed. "Well, that's settled," she said cheerfully. "Ye'll pay in the New Year. With a bit extra, fer int'rest, which ye'll agree is on'y fair and proper."

Barnaby grinned. "You're a better businesswoman than your husband gives you credit for."

The woman winked at him. "Don' I know it!" Pleased with herself, she pushed back a lock of tumbled hair (which promptly fell back down) and led him back into the tap-room. "Now then, sir, sit yerself down. I'll 'ave a supper fer ye in a trice. Do ye think yer missus'd like a bit o' mutton stew?"

Barnaby, having seated himself, blinked up at the woman. "My *missus*? Do you mean the lady there? She's not—"

"Come now, sir," Mrs. Hanlon laughed, patting him playfully on his shoulder, "I can sniff out a married couple easy as I can a spoilt fish."

"Can you, indeed? And just what is it about that lady and me that makes your nose conclude we're wed?"

"You ain't speakin' to one another. 'Tis on'y married folk who disregard one another that way."

"Perhaps all married people disregard one another," Barnaby pointed out dryly, "but not all people who disregard one another are married."

The logic eluded the innkeeper's wife. "I ain't followin' you, sir," she said, confused.

Miranda, who'd been listening, gave a small laugh. "What the gentleman means, Mrs. Hanlon," she explained, looking up from the fire, "is that disregarding one another is not restricted to married people. It's the same as saying that all fish swim, but not everyone who swims is a fish."

"Exactly!" Barnaby smiled across at her, pleased to be so well understood. "Or one could say that all artists draw, but not everyone who draws is an artist."

"Or . . ." Miranda's eyes brightened at what began to seem like a game. "All tailors sew, but not everyone who sews is a tailor."

Barnaby actually chuckled. "All doctors bleed you, but not everyone who bleeds you is a doctor."

"That's a good one," Miranda said appreciatively. "Let me think. Ah, yes. All murderers lie, but not everyone who lies is a murderer."

Mrs. Hanlon blinked in sudden understanding. "Oh, I see now. All candles burn, but not everythin' that burns is a candle."

"Yes, that's it!" Barnaby threw the woman a warm grin.

"Good for you," Miranda applauded. Warmed in body by the fire and in mood by the game, she wanted the camaraderie to continue. "All young girls flirt," she offered, "but not all flirts are young girls."

It was an unfortunate choice, for it suddenly reminded Barnaby of something he'd momentarily forgotten: who she was. His smile faded and he turned away. "That's enough," he said sourly. "The point's been made."

Miranda's eyebrows rose. The gentleman's abrupt change of tone was a surprise. What had she said to offend?

Mrs. Hanlon looked from one to the other curiously. "Are ye sure ye ain't married?"

"No, of course not," Miranda said, her mood destroyed.

"Heaven forbid!" Barnaby muttered.

Mrs. Hanlon could hardly believe them. "Well, ye surely fooled me. I ain't never yet seen a pair look more wedded than you." She glared at them in sudden disapproval. "All I can say is ye'd *better* be wed, for I 'ave on'y one bedroom upstairs. If ye can't share it, one of ye'll 'ave to spend the night down 'ere sleepin' on a bench."

Barnaby winced. "And we all know who *that* will be," he said in glum surrender to his fate.

Thus it was that, two hours later, he found himself uncomfortably laid out upon a narrow bench in a deserted taproom under a shabby comforter, his legs hanging over one carved armrest and his head propped on the other. Above him, snug under the eaves, Miss-Miranda-Pardew-that-was was contentedly ensconced in a featherbed, warm, cozy, and probably having happy dreams of all the men she'd destroyed in the past. Of all the irritations Barnaby had suffered this day, the fact that she was luxuriously, voluptuously asleep right over his head was by far the most irritating.

He tried in vain to find a position of comfort for his weary bones, but even the blanket folded in four thicknesses under him could not soften the rigidity of the hard oak bench. "It's perfect," he muttered to himself as he shifted awkwardly onto his side only to discover that there was no place for his damnably long legs. "Quite perfect. A perfect ending to this absolutely perfect day." He'd started out this morning with an instinctive conviction that he should never have left home. How right he'd been!

· Seven ·

MIRANDA WOKE THE next morning and looked round her tiny room in confusion. She had no idea of the time; the air was too gloomily dark to permit her to guess how far the morning had advanced. But as she reluctantly edged herself out from under the two comforters that had kept her warm during the night, she promised herself that, whatever the time, she would set out as soon as possible for Wymondham. It would not do to allow her new employer to believe she was unreliable. She had to get to the Traherne establishment before Mrs. Traherne lost patience.

She'd lain awake half the night worrying about how she was to get to her destination without funds, but the morning brought with it a feeling of optimism. Someone would give her a ride. The surly gentleman to whom she was tied yesterday was evidently going in the same direction. Perhaps she could prevail upon him to take her to her destination.

In one quick leap, she rose from the bed and, shivering, ran barefoot to the little dormer window of her low-ceilinged bedchamber and peeped out. To her dismay, she found that the snow was still falling. The whole world was buried in whiteness, and here and there the wind had blown the snow into huge drifts. The view smote her like a blow. There would be no traffic on the roads today. How could she possibly manage to reach the Traherne household under these trying circumstances? It might be *days* before the roads cleared. What would Mrs. Traherne think of her if she arrived at Wymondham several days after she was expected? Miranda's fear that she'd be given the sack— a fear that had haunted her in the dark of the night but had subsided in daylight—now returned in all its nighttime power. What a dreadful fix she was in! She'd cut her ties with the past so completely that they were past mending. If she were sacked, where on earth could she go?

Her spirits had only partially recovered when she came downstairs half an hour later. She found the surly gentleman standing before the bow window of the taproom, staring disconsolately out at the deepening white cover. He did not hear her approach. This gave her the opportunity to study him while he was unaware of her doing so. He was an attractive fellow, she noted, with a broad forehead, thick hair and a spare yet powerful frame. He had an air of refinement, and he'd shown both bravery and cleverness in his encounters with the footpads yesterday. All that was to the good, as was his momentary flash of charm during the brief little game they'd played with the innkeeper's wife last evening. But for the most part, he was sullen and insulting. For some reason, he'd taken her in dislike. She couldn't help wondering why. Perhaps she reminded him of someone he disliked. Perhaps he'd suffered a recent tragedy which affected his mood. Perhaps he was ill or in pain and too brave to speak of it. One should not judge too harshly, she reminded herself, when one lacks the relevant information.

She really knew nothing about the fellow. He seemed a gentleman, but did he have a profession or a trade? Was he riding toward home on the stage or away from it? Was he married? Did he have a houseful of children depending on him? Why, she didn't even know his name!

It would be helpful, she decided, to make friends with him, especially if she intended to ask him to assist her in getting to her destination. Moreover, if they were to be forced to spend days in a deserted country inn waiting for the snow to let up, the hours would pass more pleasantly if the company were congenial. Perhaps she should try again to win him over.

She stepped over the threshold, put on a bright smile and said, "Good morning," in the most pleasant voice she could muster.

He turned from the window, startled by her abrupt arrival. At this unexpected sight of her, something in his chest flipped over. Why did the sight of her move him? he wondered in dismay. But perhaps his perturbation was caused by his not having had time to prepare his defenses. Moreover, her appearance this morning was not what he'd anticipated. In the first place, her cheeks were still flushed from a warm sleep, making her look younger than she'd seemed yesterday. Then there was her hair, no longer covered by the matronly cap; it was brushed into shining smoothness and pulled back from her face into a tight knot at the nape of her neck, giving her an air of purity he found quite inconsistent with his impression of her character. Lastly, and most unexpected of all, was the look in her eyes—a look of glowing warmth and kindness. Miranda Pardew, *kind*? Impossible!

He gaped at her, unable for the moment to speak. In her severe blue muslin gown, trimmed only with a ruffle of white at the neck and at the edges of the long, narrow sleeves, she looked so proper and prim that she almost seemed to be someone else. That the voluptuous girl of the Lydell ball could be the same person as this straitlaced woman was hard to believe, though in both incarnations he had to admit she was lovely. Utterly lovely.

But as soon as those words registered in his consciousness, he was stricken with self-disgust. This woman represented everything he despised. How could he still find her lovely? *You must watch yourself*, a voice inside him warned, *or she'll make a fool of you again*. He must give her a set-down, and quickly, to be certain she was kept at a safe distance. He drew his eyebrows tightly together into his most forbidding frown. "Did you say good *morning*?" he asked disdainfully. "It's almost afternoon. I suppose ladies in your set are accustomed to sleep away half the day."

His tone put her instantly on the defensive. "But I'm usually quite an early riser, sir. It was just that the morning was so dark, and the featherbed so warm . . ." But she suddenly realized she had no need to apologize to him. "Not that my habits are any concern of yours," she added, lifting her chin.

"Mrs. Hanlon served breakfast three hours ago," he chastised, "and I had risen more than an hour before *that*. But it's not surprising I rose early. *My* bed was not conducive to late sleeping."

"I am sorry for your discomfort, sir, but you can't blame me for the inn's meager accommodations."

He merely shrugged and turned back to the window. "That tea tray on the table is for you," he informed her. "Mrs. Hanlon brought it in when she heard you stirring."

Miranda seated herself and reached for the teapot. She was discouraged by her failure to soften him but not defeated. "Would you like to join me?" she asked, determinedly cheerful. "The water is still hot."

"No, thank you."

She sipped her tea, calmly enduring the lengthy silence. After she'd poured herself a second cup, she tried again. "Do you think the snow will stop any time soon?"

"Soon? Huh!" he snorted. "If our good luck holds, we may expect to be imprisoned here till spring."

"If that's a sample of your sense of humor, sir," Miranda retorted, "I would not care for more of it. It lacks optimism."

"Then I would suggest, ma'am, that you go and exchange pleasantries with Mrs. Hanlon. She's as full of happy optimism as a puppy with a bone. She's gone to fix us luncheon. She promises ham and cold chicken and river trout and poached eggs and potatoes and custard pudding and, no doubt, several other tidbits I've forgotten. As if one could rouse an appetite after seeing the damnable depth of the snow on the road out there."

"I think it's very kind of her to feed us so lavishly. If she's gone to such trouble, we should try to do the meal justice."

"You must suit yourself, ma'am, but I would find it very hard to swallow a bite. This situation in which we're embroiled has taken away any semblance of appetite I might have had when I started out."

"I admit that our circumstances are discouraging, but it does no good to make matters worse by sulking."

"Sulking, am I?" He threw her another of his withering looks. "If you think, Miss Pardew, that you're likely to improve the situation by bandying about insulting epithets, you're far off the mark."

"Miss *Pardew*?" She stared at him in astonishment. "You called me Miss Pardew!"

He winced. *Damnation!* he cursed in his mind. *How did I let that slip?* If he wanted to keep her at a distance, he'd made a serious error. But he was a trained diplomat; he had some experience in rectifying blunders. He quickly adjusted his facial features to express bland surprise and asked calmly, "Did I? How strange. Is that your name?"

"You must know it is. At least, it was. I have not been Miss Pardew for many years."

"Ah. Your maiden name, then?"

"Yes. I am Lady . . . er, Mrs. Velacott, now."

So she did wed Sir Rodney, then, he thought. But she denied her title. He wondered why. Aloud, he only said, "How do you do?" and made a polite bow.

"You can't put me off with foolish amenities, sir. How did you know my name? Have we met before?"

"I suppose we must have, though I have no recollection of it."

"Then how can you explain—?"

He shrugged. "The name must have popped out from some deeply buried cache of memory."

"Astounding," she murmured, eyeing him suspiciously. "In fact, almost unbelievable."

"Yes," he agreed, turning away to pretend an interest in the bleak outdoor scene, "quite unbelievable."

"You've not yet told me *your* name, sir. Perhaps, if I learned it, I could determine where and when we met."

He had no intention of telling her his name. "What of your husband, ma'am?" he asked, ignoring her request. "Will he not be concerned about your absence?"

"My husband died a year ago. I am a widow."

"Oh. I see." He took a moment to let the information sink in. His reaction to the news was confused, his feelings unclear. Was he pleased? Relieved? Sorry for her? None of those reactions was appropriate, and all of them were dangerous. *Watch yourself*, the warning voice reminded him. But, too curious about the details of her life, he ignored it and plunged ahead. "Your children, then. Will they not be worried?"

"I have no children." She studied his back intently. "Now, sir, you know all about me. And I have yet to learn your name."

He turned round. In his head, he could hear her voice as it was a dozen years earlier. She'd asked him for his name then, too. But before he'd managed an answer, she'd waved him off. *I'd rather dismiss you incognito*, she'd taunted. He could give her that same "cut direct" right now, with almost the same devastating effect, and in almost the same words. Why not? Wasn't it said that revenge was sweet? *I think, Mrs. Velacott*, he could say with cold deliberation, *that I would rather remain incognito*. He took a breath and prepared to say it. "I . . . I . . ." he began. But something took over his tongue. "My name is Traherne," were the words that came out of his mouth.

He could not believe his own ears. He'd obeyed her request as meekly as a lamb. *God curse me for a damned jellyfish!* he berated himself furiously. What was the matter with him that in the presence of this woman he became a milksop, weak and unmanned?

But she, hearing the name, gazed up at him with a beaming smile. "Traherne?" she exclaimed excitedly. "Mr.

Terence Traherne? I can't tell you how delighted I am that it's you! Who better than you can explain to your wife why I am so delayed?"

Was the woman speaking gibberish? Barnaby wondered. He couldn't make sense of a word she'd said. "I only understood one thing in that speech, ma'am, and that is that you've misidentified me. I'm sorry to disappoint you, but I am not Terence. My name is Barnaby. Terence is my brother."

But if Miranda was disappointed, the feeling was momentary. After a brief blink, she turned her gaze back upon him with an expression of renewed delight. "Then you are Mrs. Traherne's brother-in-law. How wonderful for me! Her brother-in-law can as easily be my savior as her husband."

"Your . . . savior?"

"Yes, don't you see? With you to explain to your sister-in-law exactly what happened to delay us, I'm certain she will forgive my lateness. Oh, Mr. Traherne! What luck that we happened to be traveling together!"

"*Luck*?" He eyed her in disbelief, as if she were speaking in a completely foreign tongue. "Ah, yes," he said, his voice dripping with irony, "what luck, indeed."

· Eight ·

IN THE AFTERNOON, the snow stopped. It was the only good thing to happen that day. To Barnaby, it was otherwise the worst of days, full of irritations major and minor. First, there was the news that, of all people, Miranda Pardew (or Mrs. Velacott, as she apparently wished to be called) was heading for his brother's house. The prospect of having to spend his holidays in the same house as she was a major blow. Furthermore, she told him that she was to be employed by Delia, his sister-in-law, as a sort of governess. How Delia (whom he thought of as a perfectly sensible woman and an excellent mother) could have chosen this particular candidate to help raise her charming little boys was quite beyond him. Miranda Velacott was a sharp-tongued woman without an iota of sympathy for males; she would never have been Barnaby's choice as governess for his nephews. The youngest of them, little Jamie, was a quiet, sensitive sort (reminding Barnaby painfully of himself as a child) whose personality would not thrive under the tutelage of an overbearing, sardonic, cold female. Delia would soon learn what a mistake she'd made in her choice.

Added to his blighted expectations for his holiday and his concern for the well-being of his nephews was Barnaby's vexation at the prospect of having to spend another night on that hellish bench. If it were to be only one more night, he might not have been overly dismayed, but he feared he might be doomed to that deplorable wooden "bed" for a week or more. If the weather stayed cold, the roads could remain impassable well into the new year. That possibility was worse than anything else; it meant that he would be stuck here in this tiny, uncomfortable, Godforsaken inn with no one but Mrs. Velacott for company. This journey, he thought, was fast becoming a blasted disaster!

Miranda, however, was overjoyed at the cessation of the snow. Her spirit soared as the sky cleared. "Do you think Mr. Hanlon will be able to arrange a carriage for us tomorrow?" she asked Barnaby eagerly. "Do you think the road will be passable by then?"

He was unable to answer in the affirmative, but even that didn't dampen her mood. So long as she didn't let her thoughts dwell on the encounter with the highwaymen and the loss of all her worldly possessions (and there was no point in thinking about that, since it was spilt milk), she found herself surprisingly cheerful. She truly believed that her prospects were much improved since this morning; after all, the man with whom she was marooned was her employer's brother-in-law, who would not only take her to her destination but would also provide supporting proof of her explanation to Mrs. Traherne of her late arrival. If Mr. Barnaby Traherne weren't so grumpish, Miranda would have found this experience an interesting adventure.

During the long afternoon, while she sat at the fire warming her feet and he prowled restlessly round the room, she tried to converse with him, but he, when he deigned to answer her at all, responded only in monosyllables. Bored and frustrated, she finally sought out Mrs. Hanlon and prevailed upon her to unearth a deck of cards. Then she coaxed and cajoled Barnaby so relentlessly to play with her that he at last agreed. They sat down at one of the tables, and she proceeded to teach him a game of two-handed whist that she called Hearts (because, she explained, hearts were always trump). They played a full rubber, which she gleefully won. "If there's anything I despise," he growled as he pushed back his chair, "it's a gloating winner."

"Better that," she said with a throaty giggle, "than a grudging loser."

"I do not begrudge you the rubber. The whole matter is too insignificant to make me begrudge you your petty triumph."

"Petty it may be, but even in petty matters a triumph is better than a loss." She gathered up the cards and shuffled them expertly.

"You do that very well," he said, getting up from the chair. "Like an expert, in fact. Your skill at cards, coupled with your knowledge of thieves' cant, makes me wonder about you, ma'am. Can it be that beneath the prim and schoolteacherish costume hides the heart of a card-sharp?"

"Card-sharp? *I?*" She laughed heartily at the suggestion. "I hardly think so, Mr. Traherne. My knowledge of thieves' cant consists of that one word, tongue-paddler. I'm not certain how I came to learn it. I think my solicitor once referred to himself with that term. And as for my skill at cards, it was gained by spending long hours playing with my maiden aunt, who lived with me for the past decade. We passed many a lonely evening in this mildly entertaining fashion. To make it more exciting, we kept score with make-believe money. I believe, by the time we parted, that I owed her something in the neighborhood of forty-five thousand guineas."

Barnaby had to smile. She looked so innocent sitting there, the firelight on her face, her eyes misted with memory, that his suggestion seemed ludicrous. But so did her suggestion that she'd spent a decade of her life playing whist with a maiden aunt. She may not have been a card-sharp, but neither could she make him believe that she was a spinsterish stay-at-home. What really had happened in her life? he wondered.

But he had no intention of following this line of inquiry. He did not wish to become involved in her life. He had no interest in her history nor did he want any part of her future. He'd be damned if he'd permit her to charm him and entice him into any sort of web. He would not play fly to her spider.

He changed his expression from small smile to forbidding frown. "Card games are a sinful waste of time," he growled as he got to his feet.

Startled, she gaped up at him in sheer mystification. His shifts of mood confused her. This was not the first time he'd seemed to warm to her and then abruptly turned to ice. She cocked her head and studied him quizzically. "Card games *sinful*?" she teased. "What gammon! And as far as wasting time is concerned, what have we to do with our time here but waste it? Really, Mr. Traherne, you sometimes sound like a priggish Evangelical."

"Priggish?" He raised a disdainful eyebrow. "You are very quick to skewer me with insulting epithets, ma'am. I hope you're not so contemptuous of your pupils as you are of me."

Miranda lost her patience. "I am not in the least contemptuous!" she cried, getting to her feet. "Not of you and not of my pupils. I consider myself to be a good-natured, reasonably even-tempered woman. If anyone has been contemptuous, it is you!"

"Really? It was I, I suppose, who called *you* a prig."

"I did not call you a prig. I said you sounded priggish."

"Close enough as makes no difference."

"What I said was not nearly as contemptuous as your calling me a card-sharp . . . and . . . and, this morning, a sloth. And you just called into question my attitude toward my pupils. You, sir, have been offensive to me from the first."

"That, ma'am, is just the sort of wild exaggeration I might have expected from you."

"Dash it all, why should you expect *anything* from me? You don't know anything about me. We've never met before yesterday. I know you somehow heard my name, but I have no recollection of our paths having crossed. So why should you have any expectations regarding my behavior?"

"I expect *every* lady to behave like one," he said coldly.

She stiffened in offense. "If the truth be known, Mr. Toplofty Traherne, I've tried all day, in every way I know, to be pleasant and conciliating. But you've responded to every one of my attempts with rudeness and hostility. I can't imagine why you've taken me in such dislike, but I no longer care. In fact, I've had quite enough of you. I think you'd try the patience of a *saint!*" She strode to the door of the taproom with a great swish of skirts, her head high. "Good night, Mr. Traherne. Please tell Mrs. Hanlon that I'll take supper in my room."

Later that night, having given up any expectation of falling asleep on his excruciating bench, he stared up at the shadowed ceiling-beams and reviewed the words she'd thrown at him. She'd been quite right, of course. He'd behaved like a churl. But that was exactly how he wanted to behave. No one deserved it more than she. He ought to be quite pleased with himself, for the results were just what he wished. Then why, he asked himself, was he feeling like a cad?

She came down early to breakfast the next morning, but she did not respond to his greeting. Nor would she sit at the same table as he. She took a chair at another table with her back to him. Mrs. Hanlon, when she served their eggs and bacon, looked from one to the other with speculative amusement, but tactfully said nothing.

It was a brilliant morning, the sunlight dazzling on the snow. It was the sort of morning when even adults yearn to cavort in the drifts like little children. But neither Miranda nor Barnaby would let the glorious day interfere with their stubborn antagonism. As the morning advanced, and the silence between them grew more and more awkward, Barnaby actually considered offering her an apology— anything to end the deucedly appalling silence! But he quickly persuaded himself not to surrender. He was a man, he reminded himself, and she would not again turn him into a worm.

Miranda, too, was finding the silence oppressive. As she sat at a table, trying to find distraction in a game of solitaire, she wondered how she could break the silence without injuring her pride. But Mr. Traherne was a boor and a rudesby, she reminded herself, and his surly conversation would not be a great improvement over the silence.

Before either one of them was brought to the point of surrender, there was a sound of horses neighing and sleighbells jingling in the courtyard outside. They both ran to the window. A sleigh drawn by a pair of horses was drawing up beside the door. As they watched, a middle-aged man, well protected from the cold by huge boots, a high hat, mittens and a long muffler, jumped from the seat and slogged through the snow to the doorway. "Good God!" Barnaby shouted gleefully. "*Terence!*"

Miranda watched wide-eyed as the outer door was pushed open and the man from the sleigh stomped in. Barnaby Traherne was already in the vestibule when the fellow looked up from his boots. "Ah! *Barnaby*, old fellow!" he chortled in triumphant surprise. "So I've found you at last!"

The two men embraced, pounding each other's backs enthusiastically. "You *brick!*" Barnaby exclaimed. "How on earth did you—?"

"When your coach didn't arrive at Wymondham, we were all in a stew. Then Lawrence and Honoria arrived in their sleigh, which you'll agree was the perfect vehicle for this weather, so I decided to take it and go looking for you. When I discovered the stage half buried in snow, with no one about, no sign of horses, and baggage all strewn about willy-nilly, I was chilled to the marrow, I can tell you! I've been pounding on doors ever since. Damnation, boy, you're a sight for sore eyes!" And he embraced his brother again.

"It was a scurvy pair of highwaymen," Barnaby said in explanation. "They—"

"I thought as much," his brother cut in, nodding. "Thank the Lord you're safe. Everyone at home will fall on your neck, I promise you." He took off his beaver and shook the snow from it. "I say, Barnaby, you didn't by chance come across a stray female, did you? Delia was expecting a woman she'd hired to help with the boys."

Miranda, who could not avoid hearing every word, came up to the taproom doorway. "I'm the stray female, Mr. Traherne," she said, dropping a small curtsey. "Your brother and I were on the same coach."

"Mrs. Velacott, is it *you*? What luck!" Terence strode over to her and shook her hand effusively. "So you and my brother are already acquainted?"

Barnaby and Miranda exchanged glances. "Oh, more than merely acquainted," she said. "Your brother saved our lives."

"Did he, by Jove?" Terence grinned at his brother with fond admiration.

Barnaby threw Miranda a quizzical look. Her praise had surprised him. "Yes," he said to his brother, "but only after she saved mine. She leaped upon the brigand who was holding a gun to my head. And she didn't even know my name."

"Did you indeed, Mrs. Velacott? How very brave."

"Not nearly so brave as your brother, sir. He attacked armed highwaymen with nothing but his fists, not once but several times."

"Good God!" Terence exclaimed. "You seem to have had quite an adventure. You shall tell me all about it as we ride home in the sleigh. So get your things and come along. We mustn't keep Honoria and Delia and the boys in their state of alarm any longer than necessary."

By this time, Mr. and Mrs. Hanlon had come out from the kitchen. "They 'aven't any things t' get, sir," Mrs. Hanlon said, " 'cept their outer garments."

"That's right," Barnaby said, drawing his brother aside. "I say, Terence, can you pay our shot here? Those damned miscreants made off with all of my blunt."

The matter was no sooner said than done, and a few moments later Barnaby, clad in his greatcoat and hat, was climbing up on the seat of the sleigh while Terence assisted the cloaked Miranda up on the other side. Then he jumped up beside her and flicked his whip at the horses.

They waved goodbye to the Hanlons, who stood watching in the doorway, and the sleigh glided smoothly onto the snowy road. The horse's bells jingled, the sunlight glistened and a light wind blew sprays of tingling snowflakes on their cheeks. "Isn't this a glorious day?" Terence crowed loudly, his voice echoing cheerfully in the icy air. "I must apologize for crowding you, Mrs. Velacott," he added, "but since you say that you and my brother are so intimately acquainted, you won't feel awkward being crushed between us on the seat like this."

Not even this enchanting sleighride and Terence Traherne's robust good nature could make Miranda forget her resentment of Barnaby's rudeness. "I wouldn't say your brother and I are *intimately* acquainted," she said, throwing Barnaby a disdainful glance from under the hood of her pelisse, "but I *do* know your brother well enough to be familiar with all his moods and crotchets."

Barnaby met her glance with a scornful look of his own. "Perhaps we've passed mere acquaintanceship," he said dryly. "In fact, we may have reversed the whole process. If one thinks of saving a life as the ultimate act of intimacy, one could say we've gone from being intimate to being acquaintances to being total strangers."

"I say," Terence exclaimed, throwing his brother a puzzled look, "is something amiss between you two?"

"Nothing's amiss," Barnaby said.

"Nothing," Miranda echoed with an expression of bland innocence. "Nothing at all."

· Nine ·

IT WAS JUST growing dark when they arrived at the large, ramshackle manor house that the Terence Trahernes called home. It had been built for the first Earl of Shallcross in the sixteenth century, although the subsequent earls chose to inhabit a more elegant edifice in Surrey. Lawrence had given the property to Terence as a wedding gift. It was a box-like, brick-and-stone building whose third story consisted of a row of dormers behind which a number of huge chimneys reached up to the sky like blunt fingers.

Miranda had barely time to take it in, for her two sleigh companions leaped out of the equipage as soon as it drew up to the doorway and immediately helped her down. Without waiting for the others, Terence ran up the steps and brushed by the just-emerging butler. "I found him!" he shouted loudly to whoever was within. "He's *here*!"

The butler stopped Barnaby right on the stairs and threw his arms about him in a decidedly unbutlerish embrace. "Master Barnaby," he exclaimed, "we were that anxious about ye!"

"I'm fine, Cummings," Barnaby assured him. "Just fine. See to the lady, will you?"

The butler beamed at him, gave a last pat to his shoulder and then turned to lead Miranda up the stairs. They followed Barnaby over the threshold into a large, high-ceilinged hallway facing a wide stairway. Miranda had a quick impression of dark, cobwebby beams high above and worn carpets below, but she could not properly take in her surroundings, for a veritable mob of people filled the hall. They'd rushed in from all directions and were surrounding Barnaby with effusive demonstrations of welcome. The rafters rang with joyful greetings and relieved laughter. He was embraced with raucous affection by so many men and women that Miranda could not keep count of them. Nor could she recognize the surly fellow she'd come to know. Here among his family, he seemed like someone else entirely. Kissed and patted and embraced, he was actually blushing with shy pleasure! He permitted himself to be pummelled and pulled from one to the other with smiling good grace. Not only was he receiving this loving attention with becoming modesty, but what was more astonishing, he was showing equally warm affection to each of them as he returned their greetings.

Miranda, never having experienced anything like this exhibition of familial affection, felt a twinge of envy. She had to turn her eyes from the happy scene. It was then she noticed a pretty young woman standing apart in the shadows watching the excitement, just as she herself was doing. She wondered who this other outsider might be, and if she, too, was suffering pangs of envy. At that moment, however, a plump, kindly, elderly lady took the girl's arm, drew her into the circle and introduced her to Barnaby. Barnaby bowed and kissed her hand, and the girl blushed painfully, while all the others grinned and laughed.

Suddenly the crowd was distracted by loud shouts of "Uncle Barney! Uncle Barney!" from the stairs. Two robust young boys came racing down, followed by a distracted maid who had evidently failed to keep them in tow. They in turn were followed by an excited little toddler whose stubby legs could not manage the stairs with the ease of the older boys. Barnaby stepped out of the crowd that had encircled him and opened his arms. His two older nephews leaped into them and enveloped him in excited embraces.

Meanwhile, the little fellow, suddenly taking in the milling crowd in the hallway, hid himself behind the newel post, permitting himself only to peep out with one frightened eye. "Unca *Barney*," he hissed from his hiding place, "I'm *here*! Come an' hug *me*, too!"

Barnaby set the other boys on the floor and crossed over to the stairway. There he knelt down and took the little fellow in his arms. "Jamie, lad," he whispered in the child's ear, "I've missed you so!"

Miranda found herself oddly touched as she watched Barnaby swing the child up on his shoulders. She would never have guessed that the ill-mannered fellow with whom she'd passed the last three days was such an affectionate family man!

Meanwhile, the noisy arrival of his sons reminded Terence of Miranda's presence. Taking his two older boys by the hand, and motioning Barnaby to follow with Jamie, he approached the doorway where she was standing. "Mrs. Velacott," he said proudly, "I'd like you to meet your new charges." And while everyone turned and stared at her, Miranda stepped forward to face her future.

The two older boys, gazing up at her curiously, were strapping, well-built fellows, quite like their father. The little one, happily settled on his uncle's shoulder, was too preoccupied in nuzzling his uncle's ear to pay any attention to her. Terence made a sweeping gesture encompassing all of them. "This one," he indicated with a finger, "is George. He's twelve but likes to think he's fifteen. And the one with the dirty nose is Maurice—we call him Maury—who's ten. And the little fellow sitting on Barnaby's shoulder is James Lawrence Stephen Traherne, six years old, whom we call Jamie."

"George, Maury and Jamie," Miranda smiled, bowing to them, "how do you do?"

"Mrs. *Velacott*!" a ruddy-faced, middle-aged woman exclaimed, coming forward with an outstretched hand. "I didn't even know you'd come! Terence, you blockhead, why didn't you *tell* me?"

"Sorry, my dear. Too much excitement. Mrs. Velacott, this of course is my wife, Delia Traherne. And while I'm at it, I may as well make the others known to you. Standing behind Mrs. Traherne is my brother Harry. Next to him is his betrothed, Lady Isabel Folley. To my left, here, is my sister-in-law, Lady Honoria and, beside her, her husband, my eldest brother, Lawrence, the Earl of Shallcross. Finally, hiding behind them like a violet among the leaves, is their guest, Miss Olivia Ponsonby. Come out, Livy, and say hello to Mrs. Velacott, our new governess."

Miranda made her bow to his lordship and his lady, and then bowed to all the rest of them, trying hard to remember which name matched each face. She knew Barnaby and Terence, of course, and she would not mistake her new mistress, Mrs. Delia Traherne, whose ruddy, full cheeks and warm brown eyes made her seem friendly and open-hearted. The others would also be recognizable if she picked a distinctive characteristic for each as an identification. The Earl, for example, was the easiest to remember, for he had a remarkable head of wild white hair. She guessed him to be about fifty years old, but his hair made him look more like Barnaby's father than his brother. His wife, Honoria, a plump, pleasant-looking matron, had given a first impression of gentle warmth, but she was now staring at Miranda with the strangest kind of intensity. Miranda would have liked to ask the lady why, but she had to concentrate on the others if she was to identify them properly. Lady Honoria's guest, Olivia, was the youngest of the circle, certainly not more than twenty-two, and very lovely to look upon, with softly waving golden hair, soft skin and soft, frightened blue eyes. Harry, Barnaby's second brother, tall and robust, was quite like Terence in appearance. And his betrothed, Lady Isabel, was a dark-haired, proud woman with a stiff, regal bearing. *Yes*, Miranda assured herself, *I think I can remember all their names.*

The introductions made, Delia turned to her newly-arrived brother-in-law. "Barnaby, my love, you must be exhausted. Give your coat to Cummings, and let's all go to the drawing room and have tea. Mrs. Velacott, why don't you take the boys upstairs and get acquainted? I'll have tea sent up to you."

Miranda blinked for a moment, finding it necessary to adjust to a completely new way of behaving in society. *I am not a guest*, she reminded herself. *I'm a servant. I must learn to act the part.* "Yes, ma'am," she said, making a little bow. Then she turned to George and Maury. "Come, boys. You must show me the way. And Jamie," she added, reaching up for him, "do you think your 'Unca Barney' can spare you for a while?"

Barnaby, an expression of aghast surprise passing over his face, handed the reluctant child over. It seemed to Miranda that the man felt just as startled at seeing her in the role of servant as she did. She could feel his eyes on her all the way up the stairs.

When the children and their new governess disappeared, the other guests began to move toward the drawing room. Harry pulled Barnaby out of his trance and urged him across the hall. "Come on, boy, we want to hear about your adventures. Terence is frightening little Livy with the claim that the highwayman held a gun to your head. Is that true?"

The Earl and Honoria were the last to leave the hall. Both had remained staring up the stairway in a stunned silence. "Funny, Honoria," the Earl muttered, his brow knit, "but I could swear I've seen that woman before."

Honoria fixed him with a disgusted frown. "Don't you recognize her? That's Miranda Pardew!"

"What?" The Earl eyed his wife askance. "No! *Is* it? You don't mean the chit who made mincemeat of Barnaby all those years ago, do you?"

"The very same. Dash it all, Lawrence, what is she *doing* here? Governess, indeed! Her name's Velacott, isn't it? Shouldn't it be *Lady* Velacott? You don't suppose that idiot, Sir Rodney, has impoverished himself, do you?"

"How the devil would I know if he had?" the Earl responded curtly. "I don't keep up with town gossip. Haven't for years!"

"Well, I don't like it. I don't want that vixen interfering in our lives. I have such high hopes of this holiday. Livy is an angel, and Barnaby's bound to see it if he gets half a chance."

"Perhaps he'll see it, and perhaps he won't. But I don't see what Miranda Pardew has to do with it."

"I just don't like her being here, that's all. At this very critical time, too. I've a very bad feeling about this."

"Bad feeling or not, we'd better go in to tea before they come looking for us. Do you intend to say anything to Barnaby about the Pardew chit?"

"Tell him who she is, is that what you mean?" Honoria's pleasant face tightened into worried thoughtfulness. "No, I don't think so. If he hasn't recognized her, why should we stir the waters? Let's not say a word until we must. If God is kind, perhaps we won't have to."

"I imagine God has more important matters on His mind," her husband muttered, taking her arm.

They walked slowly toward the drawing room, Honoria emitting a sigh with every step. "That deuced Pardew woman!" she muttered under her breath. "She's a *curse*. What have I ever done to deserve it?"

· Ten ·

DELIA TRAHERNE BIT her lip worriedly as she mounted the stairway to the third floor where the children and the servants had their rooms. Now that her guests were dressing for dinner, she had time to interview the new governess, but she was not looking forward to the exchange. She had no talent for interviewing and instructing servants in general, and this interview in particular, she feared, would be an ordeal.

Delia was an unaffected, sensible woman who was content with her lot in life. She had a good-natured, lusty husband, three healthy sons and a comfortable if not luxurious life, and that was quite good enough for her. She did not mind the slightly run-down house, the shabby furnishings, the not-quite-adequate staff. Not afraid of hard work, she did not require servants to do things she could perfectly well do for herself. And one of the things she'd done for herself was raise her sons. If she hadn't been laid low with a severe case of pleurisy last fall, she never would have advertised for a governess. Now that she was better, she was beginning to wonder if she'd been hasty.

What had brought on these misgivings was her feeling that Mrs. Velacott in person did not appear as satisfactory a candidate as she'd seemed in her letter. There was something about her that was too . . . too—well, there was no other word she could think of—elegant.

But, Delia told herself, the woman had only been there for an afternoon. It was much too soon to make a judgment. She would not have been quite so uneasy if it hadn't been for two peculiar occurrences: a conversation she'd had with Honoria, and a remark made by Barnaby.

The first instance had occurred over tea. Honoria had taken her aside and, with the air of a conspirator, had whispered, "Did your new governess have any references?"

"References?" The question had given Delia her first twinge of discomfort. "No," she'd answered, "but that's not surprising. This is her very first position."

"I suppose it's all right, then," Honoria had murmured. "One has to start somewhere." Then she'd stirred her tea abstractedly. "Velacott," she'd added, half to herself. "I've heard that name. I once met a Sir Rodney Velacott, I believe. Do you think she might be related to him?"

"I have no idea," Delia had responded, "but I can ask her."

Honoria's eyes had lifted with a distinct look of alarm. "No, no, don't ask her. It's not . . . not at all important."

The second instance had occurred shortly afterward. Barnaby had stopped her on the stairs. "Don't you think, Delia," he'd remarked, "that a five-year-old is too young for a governess?"

"Too young?" she'd echoed stupidly.

"The older boys can handle a governess, I think, but don't you think Jamie would do better with his mother than with a . . . a stranger? When I was his age, I know I'd have preferred to have my mother guide me through my lessons."

Delia had believed, at the time, that she understood his motive. She'd patted his arm fondly, remembering how young he'd been when he'd lost his own mother. "Don't worry about Jamie," she'd reassured him. "He hasn't lost me. I'll always be there."

But now she needed reassurance herself. It was a worrisome coincidence that two people had already expressed concern about the new governess, and she'd only been there three hours!

She found Mrs. Velacott in the schoolroom with the boys. Jamie had taken her hand and, in his diffident manner, was showing her his toy soldiers. (He had hundreds of them, for all the Traherne brothers had contributed their own childhood treasures to the collection.) George and Maury, who had outgrown toy soldiers, were seated at the table, drawing. "Look, Mama," Maury said proudly as she entered, "we're making a map of the house for Mrs. Velacott, so she can find her way about!"

"What a very good idea," his mother said. "Did you boys think of it yourselves?"

"Well, Maury was trying to describe how the passage-ways connect," George explained, "and it occurred to me that a map might be clearer. I'm doing the first floor, and he's doing the second."

"An' I'm showing her my thojerth," Jamie said with his pronounced lisp. "*All* of them."

"Heavens!" his mother laughed, ruffling his hair. "Surely not every one! But you must give Mrs. Velacott to me for a while, Jamie boy, for I want to show her her bedroom. Do you think you can play with your 'thojerth' by yourself?"

"I'll keep an eye on him," George said importantly. "You ladies can go along."

Delia led Miranda a short distance down the hall. "Jamie's room is just next to yours, and the other two are across the hall," she explained as she opened the door.

"Yes, I know," Miranda said. "George already drew the sketch of the third floor for me."

"How very clever of him," Delia said proudly as Miranda stepped over the threshold and looked about her new abode. It was a small room (much smaller than the writing room Belle Velacott had offered her in the London house), with a low ceiling and a single dormer window. The furnishings were drab and spartan: a narrow bed, a dressing table and chair, a commode and a highboy—nothing as fine as a Queen Anne four-poster or a Sheraton inlaid-tile desk. But the bed had been freshly made, some Christmas greens had been set in a vase and the window cleaned to a sparkle in preparation for her arrival—all signs that Mrs. Traherne had tried to make her feel welcome. That was more than could be said for Belle Velacott.

"I hope this is satisfactory, Mrs. Velacott," Delia said, following her in.

"Yes, quite. But do call me Miranda. Mrs. Velacott is so very formal."

"Thank you, I'd like that. But only when we're private, of course. It wouldn't do for the children to hear such an informal address." She looked about her with some dissatisfaction. "I know this room isn't very spacious, but it's the only room near the boys. If you wish, we can go through some of the unused rooms downstairs after the holidays, and you can choose some pictures for the walls. And perhaps we can find a table to fit in the dormer, for you to use as a writing desk."

"That is very kind of you," Miranda murmured, trying hard to forget the luxurious surroundings of her past.

"Please sit down, Miranda," Delia said, indicating the bed. She herself perched on the dressing-table chair. "I'm sure there are many things we must ask each other."

"Yes, I suppose there are."

"For instance, do you understand your exact duties?"

"I think so. You outlined them in your last letter. Lessons in the morning, outdoor activity in the afternoon, weather permitting. George must be prepared for his entrance to school next year; I'm to tutor him in history, French and basic calculation. Maury must be helped with penmanship and spelling. And Jamie is to work on conquering his lisp and to start reading."

"Yes, that's it. And a bit of instruction in drawing would not be amiss, and some guidance in social deportment. I think, from this quick observation of you, that none of this will be beyond your capabilities."

"Thank you." She peered at Mrs. Traherne keenly. "But there is something else, isn't there?"

"Yes." There was an awkward pause. Delia's hands, resting in her lap, clenched. "To be honest, Miranda, although your letter was the most impressive of all I received, in person I find you . . ." She hesitated, not knowing quite how to go on.

Miranda looked up in alarm. "I am not what you expected? I have disappointed you, is that it? What is it, Mrs. Traherne? Am I too old?"

"Old? Oh, dear, no. What a ridiculous thought! You can't be much beyond twenty-five!"

"I am twenty-nine," Miranda admitted.

"I would not have found you too old at *forty-nine*, my dear. I myself am past forty but not yet too old to instruct my boys."

"Then what is it? Something improper in my appearance—?"

"You have a most appealing appearance, I assure you. But there *is* something about you that seems . . . well, unsuited to the position."

"Unsuited? How?"

"It's hard for me to put my finger on it. I'm not very good with words. But you look so . . . so . . . distinctive, and your carriage is so very proud . . . and even the gown you're wearing—it's quite well cut and of a very fine poplin, is it not?" She looked across at her new employee with a frank, direct gaze. "You're not running away from something, are you, Miranda? Using my household as a place to hide away from some problem in your life? *Playing* at being a governess, perhaps?"

Miranda's heart began to pound fearfully in her breast. What was Mrs. Traherne getting at? "My gown is four years old, ma'am, made for me in better days. I admit that I've seen better days. Does that disqualify me?"

"Only if it makes you dissatisfied with your position. If you have been used to elegance and luxury, how will you stand taking simple meals with the boys in the schoolroom? Or dining in the servants' hall? How will you bear taking orders from someone to whom you feel superior?"

Miranda gasped. "Oh, my Lord!" she said, horror-stricken. "Have I given the impression that I feel superior to you?"

"No, no," Delia said kindly, leaning forward and patting her knee. "Do not look so alarmed. It was only that your *yes, ma'ams* came so awkwardly to your tongue."

Miranda felt tears spring to her eyes. She got up from the bed and went to the little window, wiping at her cheeks surreptitiously. "It's true. What you say is very t-true! I am not accus . . . accustomed . . ." And to her shame, she burst into tears.

Delia jumped to her feet. "Oh, my *dear*," she exclaimed, coming up behind her new governess and putting an arm about her shoulder, "I never meant to upset you so. How you say *yes, ma'am* is . . . is such an unimportant little thing—"

"No, it's n-not a little thing," Miranda sobbed. "I am a s-servant. I m-must get used to it."

"Must you? You're obviously accustomed to servants of your own. Would it not be easier to forget this adventure and return to your old life?"

"You don't understand. This is not an *adventure* to me. I *can't* return!" She dashed the tears from her cheeks and turned to face her employer. "I'm not playing games, ma'am, truly I'm not. I have not a penny in the world. I *must* succeed at this!"

Delia, her motherly heart touched, pulled a handkerchief from her pocket and wiped the younger woman's cheeks. "Please, my dear, don't weep. I haven't any intention of discharging you if you truly mean to take your employment here seriously." She studied the other woman's tear-stained face with sympathetic concern. "You wrote that you are a widow. Was Sir Rodney Velacott your husband?"

Miranda's eyes widened. "Yes. How did you—?"

"My sister-in-law Honoria wondered about it. The name is not commonplace, you know." Delia went thoughtfully back to her seat. If this peculiar relationship was to work— and she wanted it to work, for by this time she quite liked Miranda Velacott—it would be best to encourage complete honesty. "Then you should be called *Lady* Velacott, should you not?" she prodded.

"Yes." Miranda threw Delia a shamefaced glance and turned back to stare out the window. "I didn't wish to lie to you, Mrs. Traherne, but I just didn't think the title was suitable under the circumstances. My husband's property— what was left of it after his gambling debts were paid—went to his brother. I had to find a way to support myself. But who would hire a governess with a title? Can you imagine yourself saying, 'This is her ladyship, my governess'? So I simply dispensed with it. What need have I for it? The blasted title pays no bills, nor does it put a roof over my head. It is nothing but a burden to me."

"Yes, I see." Delia nodded, her mind made up. "So you still wish to be *Mrs.* Velacott, governess to my sons?"

Miranda, hearing the acceptance in Delia's voice, wheeled around. "Yes! Oh, yes!" She flew across to Delia's side and dropped down on her knees beside the chair. "I already adore your little boys," she said, taking one of Delia's hands in hers. "I will be the very best governess to them! And I'll learn to say my *yes, ma'ams* just the way I ought, I promise you!"

Delia smiled and squeezed her hand. "Heavens, woman, who cares for that? You may call me Delia, if you like. All I want is for you and the boys to be happy together." With a relieved sigh, she got up and went to the door. "I'm glad this is all settled, Miranda. Now that I understand you, I'm sure we shall deal famously together."

Miranda got to her feet. "I think I'm very fortunate in my choice of employer," she said gratefully. "Thank you, ma'am."

Delia looked over her shoulder and grinned. "That *ma'am* was very well done, but call me Delia. It's more comfortable."

Miranda smiled back. "Thank you, ma'am, but I have no intention of overstepping my place. I'll call you Delia, if you like, but only when we're private."

· Eleven ·

DINNER WAS A raucous family affair, as it always was when the four brothers reunited. The food was abundant, the atmosphere relaxed, the company noisily cheerful. The ladies listened and laughed as the brothers threw taunts and questions at each other. Delia and Honoria, accustomed to the family patterns, smiled indulgently as the Earl, Terence and Harry vied with each other for center stage. The three older brothers still made it difficult for Barnaby to finish a sentence, but Barnaby had learned, over the years, to get his points across with a quick quip. He could now hold his own.

Tonight the teasing began with a discussion of the Earl's new sleigh. "Clever of you, Lawrence," Terence remarked, "to buy yourself a sleigh. Barnaby wouldn't be sitting here tonight if you hadn't."

"It cost a devilish long price, I can tell you," the Earl bragged. "I ordered it from a sleigh-maker in Russia. The Russians call it a *troika*, goodness knows why."

"Because they use three horses to pull it," Barnaby said.

"Listen to the boy," Harry taunted. "Showing off his foreign-office erudition."

"Not having any yourself, you're jealous that the boy has some erudition to show off," Lawrence rejoined in Barnaby's defense. "But as far as *troika* is concerned, I did perfectly well with only two horses."

"If I were the Earl, and well able to afford a stable full of horses," Terence said, to needle his elder brother, "I'd do as the Russians do and harness three."

"If I were the Earl—" Barnaby began.

"If you were the Earl," Harry cut him off, "you wouldn't buy a sleigh at all. You'd give the money to the poor and walk."

"And if you were the Earl," Barnaby rejoined, "you'd buy *two*."

Everyone, knowing Harry's tendency to extravagance, guffawed. Even his affianced bride, who hardly ever relaxed her dignity enough to smile, laughed heartily.

Conversation slowed when the lamb roast was brought to the table, smelling of rosemary and basil and other fragrant herbs. Honoria's earlier tension eased as she watched Barnaby making conversation with the quiet Olivia Ponsonby, seated at his left, and helping her to a slice of lamb. For Barnaby to show such attention to the girl was a hopeful sign. He seemed to *like* little Livy!

It gave Honoria particular satisfaction to see that all the brothers at the table this evening were paired with suitable females. This was the first time since she'd known them that this was true. Of course, the pairings were in various stages of maturity: she and Lawrence, now married for three decades, were an old couple; Delia and Terence were also well established in their fifteen-year marriage; Isabel Folley had managed to catch the elusive, forty-one-year-old bachelor, Harry, who looked happy enough in his newly forged chains; and, if all went well, Barnaby would discover in the sweet young Livy a promising partner for life. Honoria looked at the faces round the table, all smiling and aglow in the light of the branched candles at the center, and her heart filled with happy optimism. *By this time next year*, she said to herself hopefully, *all four brothers may be married men!*

She would not have been so optimistic if she'd heard what Barnaby had whispered to Delia just a few moments before. Barnaby, sitting to the right of his hostess, had leaned over and asked something that had been puzzling him. "I say, Delia, is Mrs. Velacott ill?"

"Mrs. Velacott? No, of course not. Why do you ask?"

"She isn't here at table."

"But Mrs. Velacott isn't a guest, you know, Barnaby," Delia'd whispered back. "A governess usually takes breakfast and luncheon with her charges and dines in the servants' hall after they've been put to bed, didn't you know that?"

Barnaby was startled. "No, I didn't. Is that how it's done? But, Delia, she's not . . . that is, a governess is not like a chambermaid, is she? Is it right to treat her so?"

Delia had scrutinized her youngest brother-in-law with shrewd amusement. "Can it be, Barnaby Traherne, that you're *taken* with the new governess?"

"Don't be silly," Barnaby had said quickly, his mouth tightening. "As a matter of fact, I don't like her at all. We got on so badly in the few days we were thrown together that I'm relieved to learn she's not to spend her evenings in our company. I was only curious about the . . . the proprieties."

"The proprieties, eh? I see. Well, I hope I've satisfied your curiosity. I must warn you, though, that Mrs. Velacott *will* be joining us for dinner the day after tomorrow. The boys always dine with us at Christmas Eve dinner, so she will, too."

Barnaby had pretended to indifference, shrugged and turned to smile at Miss Ponsonby at his other side. "Do have a slice of the lamb," he'd urged the young girl. "It's smothered in herbs and quite delicious."

Later, when the ladies excused themselves, and the four brothers gathered at the head of the table with their brandies, the Earl cleared his throat in an avuncular way that the others knew presaged a scolding. "See here, Barnaby Traherne," he said sternly, "I didn't wish to berate you in front of the ladies, but from what Terence told me of your encounter with the highwaymen, it seems to me you acted very rashly."

"Rashly?" Barnaby asked in sincere innocence.

"It seems you attacked the armed felons not once but twice! Attacking an armed man even once when one has no weapon seems rash to me."

"And to me," Terence added.

"And me," Harry also added.

"It wasn't rash," Barnaby said, looking from one to the other in disgust. "On both occasions I had an opening. I did exactly what you would have done in those circumstances."

"You flatter us," Harry said dryly. "I would have been shaking in my boots. And Terry would have run for cover at the first sign of an opening."

"Oh, very likely," Barnaby sneered. "Then it was not you who, before my admiring eyes, ran into a burning stable to save a horse? Or you, Terry, who dived into the lake at Shallcross to save me from drowning, and you couldn't even swim?"

"Just because they've been rash from time to time," the Earl said, "doesn't excuse you, boy! I expect better sense from you."

"Dash it all, Lawrence, I'm not a boy!" Barnaby snapped. "I'm quite old enough to know what I'm doing. And I'm here, alive and well. So let's have done with this nonsense."

"Nonsense?" the Earl said, glaring at his youngest brother in offense. "Since when do you speak to your elders in that tone?"

"Since I reached maturity," Barnaby retorted.

"The fellow's right," Harry said placatingly. "Let's be honest. If any one of us had been robbed of a gold watch and a fob to which we were sentimentally attached, we'd have put up a fight, just as Barnaby did."

"And you'd probably have beaten them," Barnaby said ruefully, "not failed miserably, as I did."

"They took your fob?" the Earl asked, suddenly sympathetic. "The one I had made for you?"

Barnaby nodded glumly.

Terence stared into his brandy-glass thoughtfully. "I think, Harry, that you and I ought to—"

"Yes!" Harry's eyes brightened. "We ought to ride out tomorrow and find those footpads."

"Right!" Terence grinned. "I've a new pistol I'm eager to try out. Those miscreants would make a most satisfactory target. With any luck, we can restore the fob to its rightful owner by Christmas."

"That is a very good idea," the Earl said approvingly, lifting his glass to them.

"*What*?" Barnaby glared at each of them in fury. "Do you think it is *still* necessary to fight my battles for me?"

Harry and Terence exchanged surprised glances. "Well, we *always*—" Harry began.

"We *like* to—" Terence muttered.

"After all," the Earl put in, "you *are* our baby brother—"

"*Damnation*!" Barnaby cursed, jumping to his feet. "Every time we get together we revert to our old ways! This must stop! I am past thirty and, I believe, completely competent to run my life. You will *not* call me baby, and you will *not* fight my battles! Is that clear?"

Under his furious glower, the Earl dropped his eyes. "We didn't mean to impugn your competence, Barnaby," he mumbled.

"We only wanted to help," Harry muttered.

"To show you what you mean to us," Terence said in meek apology.

"Affection, that's all it is," Harry added.

"That sort of affection could smother me to death," Barnaby said, refusing, for once, to surrender his anger. "I will take care of the highwaymen myself, in my own way at my own time. And if any one of you dares to interfere in this matter in any way, I'll show you how well this baby brother has learned to use his fists!"

The ladies, meanwhile, were having an entirely different sort of conversation. "Did you know, Honoria," Delia asked as soon as they'd seated themselves in the drawing room, "that Lady Isabel is quite talented on the pianoforte? Isabel, would you consent to play for us?"

Isabel nodded in gracious acquiescence, sat down at the instrument, spread her blue Persian silk skirt, closed her eyes and began to play. Her fingers moved expertly on the keys and her breast heaved with great emotion. Delia sat listening, enthralled, but Honoria had other things on her mind. She glanced over at Livy Ponsonby, who was sitting on a sofa, her hands folded in her lap and her eyes lowered. In her soft plum-colored jaconet gown and with her hair tied up on her head with silver ribbons that permitted bouncy blond ringlets to frame her face, Livy seemed as exquisite as a Sevres figurine. Honoria, disregarding the music, took a place beside Livy on the sofa. "Tell me, my dear," she whispered in the girl's ear, "what do you think of our Barnaby?"

A high color rose on Livy's cheeks. "What do I think of him?" she echoed timorously.

"Yes. You don't find him forbidding, do you? I've heard that some young ladies have described him so."

"Forbidding? Oh, no! No."

"Do you have *any* impression of him?" Honoria pressed.

The girl threw her an agonized look, like a young pupil who didn't know the location of India on the map. "I . . . I . . . think he is very kind."

"Kind?" Honoria's face clouded. "Kind" was not a word a romantic young female was likely to use to describe a man she was dreaming of.

"And good-natured," Livy added hastily.

"Yes?" Honoria urged, wanting more.

"And handsome," the girl offered, lowering her eyes and twisting a golden curl round a nervous finger. "Very handsome."

"Ah, yes." Honoria leaned back against the cushions and smiled placidly, satisfied at last. "He *is* handsome, isn't he?"

· Twelve ·

NOT LONG AFTER enduring the embarrassing questions Lady Shallcross had thrown at her, Livy Ponsonby pleaded exhaustion and retired to her room. In listless silence, she allowed her abigail to undress her. Then she excused the girl and fell weeping onto her bed. The day had been a long, horrid ordeal. To be forced to make conversation with strangers was a dreadful strain for someone as shy as she. *Dash it all, Mama*, she cried to herself, *why did you make me come*?

But she knew why. Her mother wanted her to make a good match. "You will never have a better chance," her mother had told her repeatedly in the week before she was sent from home. "Barnaby Traherne is a catch worthy of a Ponsonby. How lucky you are to have been invited! You have your aunt Jane to thank for that. You'll have a whole fortnight in which to attach him, and there'll be no other rival on the premises, either. You'll have the field all to yourself."

What her mother didn't say was that sending Livy off for a fortnight was also a way to separate her from the one man in the world with whom she was not shy: her Neddy. Ned Keswick loved her. Ned Keswick wanted to marry her, but her mother would not hear of such an "entanglement," for Ned was guilty of the very worst of sins: he was in trade.

"You are a fool, Livy," her mother had declared vehemently, "if you think Ned Keswick is a suitable husband. You are a Ponsonby, remember, not an East End nobody. You can win yourself a peer of the realm, if you set your mind to it. Yes, you can, even if you don't have a clever tongue. Don't look at me that way, Livy! I know whereof I speak. Cleverness isn't important for a girl. You're a beauty—everyone says so, not only your mother. Beauty is the only important quality a girl needs, and you have it. I won't have you throwing yourself away on that . . . that cotton merchant!"

The memory of these harangues brought on a fresh flood of tears. Ned Keswick was a dear. Positively a dear. And when he'd kissed her in the moonlight, that night less than a month ago after the Assembly dance, she thought she'd swoon in delight. He'd declared his love for her that very night, and in answer to his demands, she'd sworn to be true to him forever!

But now she'd met Barnaby Traherne, and she found herself utterly confused. Barnaby was awesomely handsome and charming, just as Mama had said he'd be, and he'd smiled at her very kindly at the table this evening. She liked him quite well. Was her mama right? she asked herself, sitting up in bed and wiping her eyes. Was her feeling for Neddy just a girlish infatuation? If Barnaby should take her in his arms in the moonlight, would she feel like swooning in delight?

And could she really win him? She'd heard rumors that other girls had found him formidable, even frightening. But he'd been very kind to her. Capturing him would certainly be, as Mama said, a feather in her cap. Why, all her friends would be green with envy!

But if she became betrothed to Barnaby, how could she explain herself to Neddy? He would accuse her of breaking her vow. He positively would! And he would have every right to hate her for it. She could not bear to have Neddy hate her!

The tears began to flow again, and she threw herself

WINTER WONDERLAND

down and buried her face in the pillows. All this was very bewildering. Making decisions had never been easy for her. This was not the first time she'd found life almost too much for her, but before when she was troubled, she'd been able to count on her mother to tell her what to do. Here, however, she had no one to guide her. It wasn't fair! Mama should never have forced her to come. *Oh, Mama,* she wept in lonely bitterness, *how could you have done this to me?*

On the floor above, Miranda, too, had retired early and then found that she could not sleep. Excited by the challenge of her new post, her mind made plan after plan of ways to tutor her charges. At last, convinced that sleep was still a long way off, she rose from her bed. Shivering from the cold, she wished she had the warm dressing-gown she'd packed in her now-lost portmanteau. But, having nothing else to put over her nightdress (generously given to her by one of the maids), she covered herself with her cloak. Then she lit a candle and made her way down the hall to the schoolroom.

The room was as the boys had left it: the table littered with picture-books and drawings, the floor covered with scattered toy soldiers. Evidently, the housemaids were too busy helping with the dinner downstairs to have had time to clean the schoolroom. Miranda threw back her cloak, pushed up the sleeves of the muslin nightdress and set to work herself, piling the papers and books on one side of the table and then bending down to pick up the toy soldiers. It wasn't the first time she'd done housemaid's work, she told herself ruefully, nor would it be the last.

A number of the little soldier-figures, she noticed, were grimy from sticky fingers. She laid them on the table, found a piece of cloth, sat down and set to work cleaning them. As she worked, she took a close look at the figures. They made a motley collection; some of them were roughly carved of wood, while others were carefully sculpted and cast in brass or fashioned from metal she could not identify, but all were colorfully painted, each detail of the uniforms carefully re-created. Some, from which the paint had faded or had been partially rubbed off, she set aside. Touching them up with fresh paint would make an enjoyable pastime for the boys on a rainy day, she decided.

Suddenly something made her look up. Standing in the doorway, studying her with a puzzled expression, was Barnaby Traherne. "Oh!" she said, startled.

"Good evening," he said, eyebrows raised questioningly.

She got to her feet, feeling awkward, like a housemaid caught trying on her mistress's jewels. "Good evening," she muttered, blushing as she drew her cloak around her.

"You needn't get up for me," he said, his eyes taking in her strange costume and her hair, which she'd plaited into one long braid. "You're not a housemaid, you know."

"Close enough as makes no difference, to use one of your own expressions," she said with a sudden smile.

He did not smile back. "I'm sure my sister-in-law does not intend for you to do the cleaning."

"I want to do it. I couldn't sleep, and this seems as good a way of tiring myself as any."

"I'm not sleepy, either," he said, stepping over the threshold. "May I help?"

"I'm sure your sister-in-law does not intend—"

He put up a hand to silence her. "You seem to enjoy throwing my words back in my face. Have your new duties had no effect on your saucy tongue, ma'am?"

She made a little housemaidish curtsey. "I do beg your pardon, sir. I shall try to remember my place and curb my tongue. Do sit down, if you truly wish to engage in so lowly an occupation—and can find yourself a polishing cloth."

"I'll take half of yours," he said, putting down his candle beside hers and ripping the cloth in half.

They sat down and began to work. "You couldn't have come up here with the purpose of helping me with this polishing," she said. "Was there something you wanted?"

"Well, yes," he admitted, throwing her a quick, embarrassed glance. "I didn't see you at dinner, and I couldn't help wondering whether . . . that is, Delia wondered . . ."

"Yes?"

"If your dinner was . . . er . . . satisfactory, down in the servants' hall."

"*Delia* wondered?"

"Yes," he lied.

"Why would you, or she, be concerned about such a thing?"

"Well . . ." He fixed his eyes on the soldier in his hand and polished away vigorously. " . . . you are not accustomed to dining with servants, are you?"

She stared at him in some surprise. He'd somehow sensed that she'd come down in the world, and he was evidently disturbed by the fact that she was required to dine with the servants. She could not help but be touched by his sympathy. "Of the many new experiences I must grow accustomed to," she assured him gently, "that one is the least difficult. But thank you—and Delia—for your concern. You may rest assured the servants' hall is cheerful, the staff friendly and the meals generous."

"Good," Barnaby said.

She peered at his bent head. "It was kind of you to ask."

"Hmmph," was his response.

They worked in silence for a while. "These soldiers are quite old," he remarked at last. "I used to play with them when I was a boy, and so did my brothers."

"Speaking of your brothers," she said thoughtfully, "you seem to be very attached to them. And to their families. That is quite astonishing to me. I had not thought of you as the affectionate sort."

"Hadn't you? Why not?"

She threw him a hesitant look across the table. "If I answer, you will only scold me for my saucy tongue."

"I promise not to. Tell me."

"Because . . . because you behaved so boorishly to me during our sojourn at the inn."

He lifted his head in offense. "I take umbrage at the word

boorish. I was in no way boorish."

"Oh? What word would you use?"

He thought for a moment. "Formal. I was trying to keep a formal distance."

"Why?" she asked bluntly. "I can see why you might feel a need to be formal here, where I am a servant and you are a guest. But why was there a need, at the inn, to be so distantly formal?"

He stared at her then, trying to formulate an answer. The question, he realized, was fortunate, because it reminded him of the *real* reason he'd kept his distance. He'd forgotten it again. She looked so lovely with the candlelight throwing a mellow glow on her cheeks and the curves of her throat, shining in her eyes and making a glinting treasure of her hair, that it was easy to forget himself. Sitting opposite her like this and speaking together with comfortable ease made her seem like an old acquaintance. If she hadn't asked the question, it would have slipped his mind completely that she was Miranda Pardew, the nemesis of his youth.

Of course, he wouldn't admit that aloud. He had to find an excuse for what she justifiably interpreted as boorishness. "We were strangers, after all," he hedged, "thrust together by circumstances, not our own wishes. It would not have been proper to . . . to . . ."

"To relax into friendship?" she suggested. "Would that have been improper?"

"I think so, yes."

"Then I suppose I am not as proper as you. Your standards are too exacting for me."

"Too exacting?" He threw down his cloth and rose. "You are implying that I am a prig. If memory serves, you said that once before."

Startled, her eyes flew up to his face. "I *never* said—! I didn't *at all* mean to—!"

"Never mind. Our standards of behavior *are* very different. You are bound to think of me as priggish, just as I am bound to think of you as . . . as . . ."

"Saucy?" she offered.

"Yes, I suppose that word will do as well as any." He picked up his candle and went to the door. There he paused. "The reason I came up here seeking you tonight, Mrs. Velacott, was to offer my assistance if, in your new position, you should run into any difficulties. Despite my priggishness, that offer holds. Good night, ma'am."

Before Miranda could respond, he was gone, leaving only a quickly disappearing circle of candlelight behind him. She gaped at the empty doorway, dumbfounded. She would never understand him. One moment he was sitting opposite her, charming and friendly and apparently concerned for her welfare, and the next he was withdrawn, cold and forbidding. Was it something she'd said? Had her teasing him about being too proper touched some sort of sensitive spot? He was a mystery.

With a sigh, she picked up her piece of cloth and resumed polishing. She did not wish to trouble her mind about the mystery of Barnaby Traherne. The strange Mr. Traherne was not her concern. She tried to turn her mind back to planning lessons for her three pupils, but her thoughts kept returning to the man who'd just sat opposite her. What was it about him that bothered her so much? she asked herself. And, astoundingly, the answer popped into her head with the shining clarity of true insight: what troubled her most about him was her sense that, when he looked at her, he was seeing someone else. Someone else entirely.

· *Thirteen* ·

BARNABY CAME DOWN to breakfast the next morning feeling out of sorts and dejected by the gloomy weather that would not go away. Though it was not snowing, the dark sky and icy wind persisted. It was a day in which no one was likely to venture out-of-doors. There would be no riding, no brisk walks, no outdoor games. There would be nothing to do all day but play billiards and cards, neither of which he particularly fancied.

He was not surprised that no one was yet at breakfast—it was a perfect day to stay late abed. Although Cummings offered to serve him his favorite shirred eggs or a bowlful of hot porridge (which, the butler said, "would sustain him mightily on such a dreadful morning"), he refused, not wishing to eat alone. Instead, he wandered off to the library. It was there he discovered someone even more unhappy than he: Livy Ponsonby, who stood at the window, crying.

He'd gone halfway across the floor to the bookshelves before he saw her. He stopped in his tracks in embarrassment. "Oh! I beg your pardon, Miss Ponsonby," he said, backing toward the door. "I didn't mean to intrude."

She took a quick glance round, colored, and then turned away again, lowering her head and brushing away her tears. "You d-don't intrude, sir," she managed, her light, girlish voice choked. "You have as much r-right here as I. More, in fact."

Something in her tone made Barnaby pause on the threshold. It seemed to him that the girl might actually desire a little companionship. "I'd hoped we had reached less formal terms than *sir* and *ma'am*," he said gently. "Can you not call me Barnaby?"

"But just now you c-called me M-Miss P-Ponsonby, didn't you?" she accused, throwing him a tearful little smile over her shoulder.

"I apologize for that. Olivia you shall be from this moment on."

She turned round to him. "Livy, please." She looked quite appealing in a figured-muslin morning dress with a neat white tucker and long sleeves puffed at the top. Her gold ringlets were pinned up at the top of her head in tousled charm, and her lips were swollen from her weeping. A man would be a churl not to wish to comfort her.

In this instance, Barnaby was no churl. "Livy, then," he said, smiling at her. He crossed the room to the window where she stood. "You were crying, Livy. Is something amiss?"

She shook her head. "I am a silly wetgoose. It was only . . . only . . ."

He took her elbow and guided her to an easy chair near the fire. "Only—?"

She lowered her lovely blue eyes. "Only that I was feeling lonely."

"Oh, is *that* all?" He perched on the hearth before her and grinned. "In an hour or less, the whole family will come tumbling down the stairs in various states of undress demanding their breakfasts, and the din will be so great you'll find yourself wishing to be lonely again."

She gave a hiccuping laugh and then, astoundingly, burst into tears again. "You don't understand," she wept. "You're such a jolly, c-close, af-f-fectionate family. Seeing you laugh and joke together as you do m-makes me miss m-mine."

"Oh, I *see*." Barnaby now fully understood her tears. The poor girl, being the only outsider in the midst of this close-knit clan, was feeling left out. "I can't say I blame you," he said, patting her hand sympathetically. "It's hard to be taken away from your family circle, especially at Christmastime."

"Yes," she admitted, wiping her eyes with an already-soaked handkerchief.

He pulled out his own handkerchief, lifted her chin and dabbed at her cheeks. "How many are there in your family?"

"Not so m-many as yours," she said, sniffing back a final sob and favoring him with a grateful, if tremulous, smile. "My mother, of course. And Papa. And my married sister, Charlotte, who always comes with her baby to spend Christmas with us, and my little sister Hetty." Her smile faded and she sighed pensively. "I've never traveled without Mama before. I m-miss her."

"Then tell me, Livy, what made you tear yourself away to come to us?"

"Mama insisted. She positively insisted."

"Did she? Why?"

"She said it was an honor that I could not refuse."

"An *honor*?"

"Oh, yes, indeed. Positively. Not many girls, Mama said, are invited to spend a fortnight with the family of someone as important—and as kind—as Lady Shallcross."

"I see." Barnaby couldn't help wondering if Honoria realized that the kindness she'd bestowed on the girl was the cause of loneliness and pain. "So, for this 'honor' you must miss Christmas at home with your mother and sisters. That *is* too bad. You have two sisters, you say?"

"Yes. I'm the middle one."

"No brothers?"

"No."

"How fortunate for you. Brothers can be a nuisance."

"Barnaby!" Livy clucked her tongue in reproof. "How *can* you say such a dreadful thing? You positively revel in each other's company, you *know* you do!"

"Yes, in truth, I do. Though my brothers can be irksome sometimes, I admit that I enjoy spending time in the family circle."

"Oh, yes. One's family circle is the very best place. Positively."

He chuckled, both amused and touched by her repetitive use of the word *positively* when her personality was not in the least positive. "Then, Livy, I shall see to it that you, too, enjoy this family circle," he said, rising and pulling her to her feet. In trying to cheer the girl, he found that he himself was feeling more cheerful. "From this moment on, you will share my brothers with me. I know that sharing my family will not be as satisfying as being with your own, but we shall make it the next best thing. Positively."

As Barnaby guided the girl to the door, intending to lift her spirits by encouraging her to take a hearty breakfast, he came face-to-face with Mrs. Velacott and her eldest charge, George. The boy's face lit at the sight of his uncle. "Good morning, Uncle Barney," he cried. "You'll never guess what we're doing."

"Then you must tell me," his uncle said, ruffling the boy's hair affectionately.

"We're studying history. We've come down to find a proper history book. Mrs. Velacott doesn't like the one I've been using." He glanced up at his governess, an expression of pride crossing his face. "She says it's too childish for me."

Barnaby eyed Miranda with raised eyebrows. "Starting lessons already? Two days before Christmas?"

"It seemed a good idea," Miranda said, feeling defensive. "The weather is not conducive to much else."

"I was not criticizing," Barnaby assured her. "Just surprised. I didn't expect you immerse yourself so promptly in your work."

"No?" she asked, lifting her chin belligerently. "Why not?"

Because I didn't think you a conscientious sort, he said to himself, but he would not make so disparaging a comment aloud—not now, in front of his nephew. So he only said, "No reason, ma'am." He stepped aside to let her by. "Are the younger boys doing lessons, too?"

"Oh, yes, indeed they are."

"Maury is writing a story in his notebook, and Jamie is practicing the letter A on his slate," George volunteered.

"Then you all are very busy, and I shouldn't keep you," Barnaby said, throwing Miranda a quizzical look before turning back to George and patting his shoulder approvingly. "But I must warn you, ma'am, that my brother's library is distressingly inadequate and idiosyncratic, despite the fact that he's managed to fill a wall of shelves. I believe the best you'll find here is Smollett's *History of England*. It might do for a while. When I return to London, I can send you something better, if you like."

"I would be very grateful, sir," Miranda said.

Barnaby nodded and, with his hand on Livy's elbow, led the girl off down the corridor.

Miranda stood gazing after them, feeling strangely irked. The man had not let go of the girl's arm during their entire conversation. Was he courting her? Miranda wondered. And what if he were? What difference could it make to her? "Come, George," she said, forcing herself to put the irritating Barnaby Traherne out of her mind, "let's find the Smollett. If his history is anything like his novels, reading it will be entertaining, even if not very accurate."

They returned to the schoolroom with three volumes of *A History of England from the Revolution to the Death of George II* by Tobias Smollett tucked under their arms. George, full of first-day enthusiasm, immediately took Volume I to the window seat and began to read, while Miranda placed the other two books on a shelf she'd cleared of toys for that purpose. Then she noticed that Jamie was not at the worktable. Instead, he was sitting on the floor in the corner, absently fingering one of his little soldiers and staring morosely into space. "Jamie," she asked, "have you finished your writing already?"

He turned his head away. "It'th on the table," he muttered.

She looked at the slate. It was covered with three rows of A's, surprisingly well executed for a first-time writer. "Why, this is excellent writing!" she exclaimed. "I'm very pleased."

"Mmmph," the child grunted, not looking up.

Puzzled at his strange reaction, she knelt down beside him. "Aren't you proud of yourself, Jamie? You should be."

"*Maury* should be proud."

"Maury?"

"He'th the one who did it."

"Maury did your work for you?"

"Yeth. Tho you can be proud of *him*, not me."

She got to her feet. "Maury, why—?"

Maury looked up from his work and shrugged. "He wasn't doing it right. You're not cross with me, are you? I just tried to help him."

"No, I'm not cross. But please let him do his own work in future. Come to the table, Jamie, and erase your slate. We'll start again. You can still be proud of—"

"No!" the child shouted, throwing his toy soldier across the room, getting to his feet and running to the door. "I can't do it. I won't be proud. I want Mama!" And, his underlip trembling, he ran out and slammed the door behind him.

Miranda stared at the door, aghast. What had she said or done that had caused this outburst? She'd been at work as governess barely an hour, and she'd already blundered. Being a governess, she realized with a sinking heart, was not going to be as easy as she'd anticipated.

· *Fourteen* ·

THE WEATHER FOR Miranda's second day as governess was quite different from the first. The air sparkled with sunshine made glistening by a brisk wind. The snowy landscape and the crisply fragrant air were too inviting for boys to be kept indoors. Besides, they had worked hard at their lessons all day yesterday. Even Jamie had returned to the table and, after much tender cajoling, had learned to read and write his name. Miranda decided they needed an outing. With Delia's permission, she instructed their nursemaid to dress them in warm jackets, boots, mittens and mufflers, and she took them outside for a couple of hours of play.

The ladies of the household, too, would probably have enjoyed an outing, but as soon as their leisurely breakfast had been consumed, they all agreed that they preferred to occupy themselves fashioning wreaths and mistletoe boughs with which to decorate the doorways, windows, bannisters and mantels. The gentlemen, on the other hand, were given an outdoor assignment: to fetch a suitable yule log from the home woods. Only Lawrence was unwilling to face the chilly outdoors. "I'm too old to chop trees and pull logs," he said, ensconcing himself in an easy chair before the sitting-room fire with a copy of *Waverly* on his lap, Sir Walter Scott being his favorite writer.

"Not too old, Your Lordship," his brother Harry taunted. "Just too high in the instep."

"Right," Terence agreed. "Taking advantage of your lordly privileges, if you ask me."

The Earl turned a page with calm deliberation. "There wouldn't be much use in lordly privileges," he said, waving them off, "if one didn't take advantage of them."

Terence, Harry and Barnaby, well protected from the cold with mufflers and wool caps, set off on their excursion with noisy enthusiasm. The task, even complicated by a great deal of snowball throwing and wrestling about in the drifts, was accomplished in less than an hour. It was not yet noon when they dragged the log to the kitchen door. Harry and Terence handed their axes to Barnaby, hoisted the six-foot-long tree trunk to their shoulders, and were just about to enter the doorway when Barnaby caught a glimpse of Jamie's red wool cap on the other side of the kitchen-garden shrubbery. "Go on ahead," he said to his brothers. "I'll be with you shortly."

He disposed of the axes and tramped round the shrubbery. There he found his little nephew sitting cross-legged on a pile of snow, his chin resting on his mittened hands and his expression glum. Jamie's teary eyes were fixed on a scene across the field, where his two brothers and Mrs. Velacott were busily making a snowman. The sounds of their laughter tinkled in the air.

"Tell me, Jamie lad," Barnaby said, dropping down beside the boy, "how can you be looking so miserable when there is all this wonderful snow lying about?"

"They're makin' *my* thnowman," the boy said, pouting.

"What do you mean? Whom are you speaking of?"

"George an' Maury. They were buildin' a fort, an' I wath makin' a thnowman. An' then the head fell off." His underlip trembled, and he wiped his dripping nose with a soggy mitten. "An' then they came an' fixthed it, an' now *they're* makin' him an' I'm *not!*"

"I see. So it won't be your snowman any more."

"No, it won't." The boy unfolded his legs, threw himself upon his uncle and buried his head in Barnaby's lap. "I never get to make anythin' by mythelf," he whined.

"That *is* too bad," Barnaby said kindly, "but it seems to be the way of big brothers. Your father and your uncle Harry did the very same sort of thing to me, when I was your age." *And they still try to do it*, he added to himself.

The child looked up. "*Did* they? Honetht and truly?"

"They certainly did. It's the curse of being the youngest."

Jamie nodded wisely. "The curthe, yeth."

"But there's something you can do about it, you know."

"There ith?"

"Yes. You can fight back."

Jamie's eyes brightened. "I can?"

"Yes, you can. Come with me, and I'll show you how it's done."

They got up, Barnaby took hold of the boy's mittened hand, and they plodded across the field to the merrymakers. "I say, chaps, that's a very fine snowman," Barnaby said when they arrived.

The boys greeted him warmly, and Mrs. Velacott gave him a polite good-day. "Do you like the chest part, Uncle Barney?" Maury asked. "George thinks it ought to be fatter."

"I really couldn't say, Maury, because the snowman's not mine. Jamie says he's the one who started it, so wouldn't you say it's really his?"

Maury shrugged. "I s'pose so. Do you want the chest fatter, Jamie?"

Jamie motioned for his uncle to bend down, and with Barnaby kneeling, the two held a quick, whispered conference. Then Jamie turned back to his brothers. "No," he said firmly. "If I want him fatter, I'll do it mythelf."

"Oh, you will, will you?" objected George loudly. "That's showing a proper gratitude, I must say."

"Why should he show gratitude?" Barnaby asked.

"Why? Because he couldn't even get the head on."

"That's right," Maury agreed. "If we didn't help, he'd have a headless snowman."

"What if I *wanted* a headleth thnowman?" Jamie demanded, showing an unusual—and, to his uncle, a welcome—belligerence.

"You didn't want a headless snowman," George insisted. "You were bawling your eyes out about it."

"That's right, Jamie," Miranda said gently. "Your brothers were only helping. It isn't right to be sullen when you should be grateful."

Jamie, not knowing how to respond, turned his eyes up to Barnaby in confusion.

Barnaby glared at the governess. "Mrs. Velacott," he said stiffly, "may I speak to you in private for a moment? And while we're conferring, Jamie, you tell George and Maury just what *you* want to do to the snowman. It's up to you to decide how they may help, if you want their help at all."

He marched off across the field, Miranda obediently following. When they were out of hearing of the boys, Barnaby wheeled around. "Have you no feelings, ma'am?" he demanded angrily. "Didn't you see that child sitting all alone on a mound of snow, his snowman usurped by bigger and stronger powers and his joy in his creation destroyed?"

"Good heavens, Mr. Traherne," she said, surprised by his vehemence, "must we have such a to-do over a snowman?"

"It is not over a snowman, ma'am, but over a method of upbringing. The child needs some understanding, and some encouragement to defend himself."

"To defend himself from what?"

"From a pair of overbearing brothers."

"You are misinterpreting the situation, sir, not having seen it from the beginning. Jamie was *crying* for their help. George and Maury are quite generous with Jamie. Protective, even. I've noticed it often. Today, they were happily building their fort when the child's crying interrupted them. They quite cheerfully gave up their own activity to help him with his. But instead of thanking them, Jamie began to whine. I cannot encourage whining."

"Perhaps, ma'am, you might consider *why* the boy was whining. Has it not occurred to you that a child can be helped *too much*? That a headless snowman a boy builds *for himself* is a greater source of satisfaction than a better one someone else builds for him?"

Miranda stared at him, her expression suddenly thoughtful. "Yes, I *see*. Of course! What you're suggesting also explains something that happened yesterday. The child's self-confidence is being weakened by too much assistance from his brothers. I hadn't thought of that."

"No, of course you hadn't," Barnaby said with withering disdain. "What can a woman who has spent her life disporting herself in the ballrooms of London be expected to know about raising children?"

Miranda, who was already berating herself for not having understood what was now so obvious, did not need another abusive voice added to her own. Every muscle in her body tensed. "*Disporting* myself? What on earth are you talking about?" she demanded angrily. "What can you know about how I spent my life?"

"I know enough," he said. "Enough to be convinced that Jamie's mother has not been very wise in her choice of governess." And with that withering set-down, he turned about and stomped off to see what he could do to assist Jamie in asserting his rights to the snowman.

Miranda stared after him, her blood pumping through her veins in furious tumult. It was not fear of losing her position that caused this turmoil, for Delia had promised to give her support while she learned her job. It was Barnaby Traherne who upset her. Why was this man, who was so kind and affectionate to everyone else, so bitterly vituperative to her? True, he'd been wiser than she in the matter of Jamie, but she'd given him his due. She'd *admitted* her lack of insight. Was her error so great as to deserve that sort of reprimand? *Jamie's mother has not been very wise in her choice of governess,* indeed! Who was he to judge? How many children had *he* raised?

He may have been in the right this once, but that was no excuse to insult her. Confound the man, he invariably managed to raise her ire! It was getting so that, every time she saw him, she had an overpowering urge to box his ears.

· Fifteen ·

A FOOTMAN HAD been sent to the abandoned stagecoach and
had recovered what was left of the baggage. For some reason,
Barnaby's battered portmanteau had not been opened, so
all the items of clothing he'd brought were restored to
him. Miranda's things, on the other hand, had been rifled
through and either stolen or scattered about. Most of her
underthings were recovered, but only two of her gowns were
returned to her. One was a shabby, gray-and-white-striped
linsey-woolsey, suitable for the schoolroom but much too
workaday for Christmas Eve dinner with the family.

Her only other dress, aside from the slate-blue kerseymere
she'd worn every day since she left home, was a green
ballgown made of lustring so luxurious that Miranda wondered why the highwaymen had not taken it. It was, in its
opposite way, as inappropriate as the linsey-woolsey, for
it had a shockingly low décolletage, a tendency to cling,
a long train, and it was trimmed at the neck, sleeves and
hem with gold-tasseled lace so exquisite that no one would
believe a governess could afford it. A particularly daring
guest might wear the gown, but a governess could not.

She was in a quandary. Tonight, Christmas Eve, was
to be festive. She had not attended a festive occasion for
years, so she felt unduly excited at the prospect of attending
the dinner. She yearned to put off the blue muslin for one

evening, but she had nothing else to wear but the ballgown. If she snipped off the tasseled lace, she wondered, and cut off the train, would the green lustring be passable? It might, she decided, if she covered her bare shoulders with a shawl.

Hurriedly, for she had very little time to spare, she made the adjustments to the gown. Then she removed her widow's cap and took down her hair. She'd worn it pulled severely back into a knot all these days, and well hidden under the cap, but tonight she would let it show. She brushed it up into the style she'd favored in her younger days; called *à la Grecque*, it required that the longer hair be caught up in the back and the shorter left free to curl round the face. Then she slipped into the gown, threw a dark green paisley shawl (the item she was most grateful the highwaymen had spared) over her shoulders and, without daring to look at herself in the mirror, ran out to gather the boys.

All three of the children were resplendent in manly coats, starched shirts and neatly folded neckcloths, their faces scrubbed and shining, and their hair pomaded into unrecognizable neatness. It was no wonder, for they'd been dressed this evening by no less a personage than Terence's own valet. She was about to exclaim over their appearance when George, taking his first glimpse of her, exclaimed, "Crikes!"

Maury stared for a moment, mouth agape, and then said, "Double crikes!"

"What does that mean?" Miranda asked, kneeling down to straighten Jamie's collar.

Jamie put his arms about her neck and whispered in her ear, "It meanth your hair is pretty."

"*Everything* is pretty," George said, beaming at her.

"Very, very pretty," Maury said, taking her hand.

"And so are the three of you. Handsome as can be in your fine coats and neckcloths. But we must remember that handsome is as handsome does. So please, Maury, don't slurp your soup. And George, make your bow to

Lady Shallcross first. Come along now, quickly. We don't want to be late."

Everyone had gathered in the drawing room for preprandial sherry. The fire crackled merrily, the wreath over the mantel looked appropriately festive, and the guests sparkled in holiday finery. Honoria, in purple velvet, sat close to the fire and sipped her drink, watching Barnaby from the corner of her eye. She was quite delighted at the attention he'd been paying to her shy little protégée, but tonight Livy looked particularly lovely, and Honoria wanted to see the effect on him. The girl was dressed in a soft, rose-colored evening gown of Florentine silk that seemed to reflect its color upon her cheeks. Her delicate features glowed in the candlelight and her golden curls made a halo round her face. If Barnaby was not completely smitten by this charmer, Honoria thought, she would have to give him up as a hopeless case.

But Barnaby did indeed seem to be admiring the girl. He was at this very moment handing her a glass of sherry and making some sort of flattering comment about her appearance, because the girl simpered and colored charmingly. As Honoria watched, however, Barnaby chanced to look across the room, and his entire expression changed. Honoria followed his glance. In the doorway stood Miranda Pardew, wearing a clinging green gown almost exactly like the one she'd worn at the Lydell ball so many years ago. *Good God!* Honoria thought. *She's almost as breathtaking as she was then, drat her!*

Barnaby must have thought so too, for the expression on his face was not unlike the one he'd had when he'd first laid eyes on her: wide-eyed adoration. Nor was he the only man in the room to react. Terence immediately crossed to her, saying, "Mrs. Velacott, you are a vision!"

Harry, who'd been seated next to Lady Isabel on one of the sofas, jumped to his feet to second the compliment, but a glance at his betrothed was enough to stay his tongue. He sank back down and said nothing.

The Earl, married too long not to know what his wife was thinking, merely exchanged a meaningful glance with Honoria. *She really* is *a vixen*, they said with their eyes.

Miranda, who recognized male admiration when she saw it, realized too late that she'd made too flamboyant an entrance for a proper governess. Her cheeks grew hot. "The *boys* are the vision," she said, gently urging them forward.

Honoria, swallowing her irritation, smiled and rose eagerly from her chair. "So they are," she said, holding out her arms to them. "Did you ever see three such handsome young gentlemen? Here, I'm going to place myself under the mistletoe, and you three must give me a kiss."

Delia and Isabel also rose and, amid much horrified squealing from the bashful Jamie and noisy laughter from the others, demanded their share of the boys' embraces. In the midst of this liveliness, Cummings came in to announce dinner. "Lawrence," Honoria ordered, "you must claim the honor of taking Livy in to dinner, since she looks so particularly lovely this evening. Livy, dear, take my husband's arm."

The Earl smiled obediently and started toward the girl's chair. As he passed his wife, he muttered sotto voce, "What are you up to?"

"I must talk to Barnaby," she whispered back. She then took it upon herself to direct the pairing-off of the rest of the group, assigning Harry to escort Delia, Terence to usher Isabel, and the three boys to see to their governess. "And you, Barnaby, may take *my* arm."

The parade passed into the dining room, but Honoria held Barnaby back. "Wait a moment," she murmured, taking him aside. "I want to talk to you."

Barnaby looked down at her with upraised brows. "You seem agitated, my dear. What's troubling you?"

"The governess, of course. Barnaby, my love, do you know who she is?"

"Yes, of course. Why do you ask?"

Honoria gasped in astonishment. "You *knew* she's . . . she's *Miranda Pardew*?"

"I knew who she was from the moment I set eyes on her on the stage. I suppose it was her appearance tonight that triggered your memory."

"Her appearance tonight, in that absolutely *shocking* gown, certainly *would* have triggered my memory, but Lawrence and I recognized her that first evening. I didn't know that you, also, knew her identity. Why didn't you say something to me?"

"What was there to say? Her identity is of no importance, is it?"

Honoria gazed up at him nonplussed. "But, Barnaby, doesn't it trouble you at all to find that . . . that *baggage* in the same house with you?"

"Not a bit. I admit to a certain curiosity about her reasons for taking a post as a governess—a post for which one would imagine she's eminently unsuited—and for dropping her title, but I am otherwise unaffected by her presence."

Those words were just what Honoria had prayed to hear. She expelled a deep breath of relief. But Miranda's presence still troubled her. "Do you think she's up to something havey-cavey?" she asked.

"If she is, I can't imagine what it could be. Why are you so distrustful of her?"

"I don't know. I never liked her. Why is she pretending to be a governess? And if she's not pretending, then what sort of governess brings her charges down to dine wearing a gown that would raise eyebrows in a ballroom?"

"Would it?" Barnaby asked innocently. "It seemed perfectly acceptable to me. Come, my dear, let's go in before the others begin to wonder what's keeping us." He took her arm and led her toward the dining room. "And as for our Miranda, what harm can she do? I wouldn't give her another thought, if I were you."

· *Sixteen* ·

EVERYONE BUT JAMIE heartily enjoyed Christmas Eve dinner. The boy, being petted, smiled at, teased and fondled by so many people all at once, became tongue-tied and uncomfortable. He kept his eyes fixed on his plate except when his parents or his governess or his uncle Barney spoke to him, and even they were rewarded with only brief, timid little answers. Poor Barnaby, seated between his bashful nephew and the bashful Livy, found himself having to work hard to draw out his dinner partners. Fortunately, Livy was by this time feeling more at home; she giggled frequently at Barnaby's quips and appeared to be enjoying herself.

After dinner, Terence, Delia and their guests gathered in the drawing room, where Lady Isabel played carols and everyone sang. Then Delia lit the Yule log with a bit of the charred remains of last year's log. Since the new log was covered with decorative greenery, it flared up in a great blaze that made everyone cheer. They settled themselves before the fire, the children stretched out on the floor, and listened to the Earl tell Christmas stories. Before they knew it, it was time to ready themselves to venture out for the midnight church service.

The older boys had been given permission to attend, but Jamie was ordered to go upstairs with his governess and get ready for bed. Unhappy at this decision, Jamie clung stubbornly to his mother's cloak and would not let go. Neither Miranda's coaxing nor Delia's firm orders would convince the child to release his hold. Finally, in disgust, Terence forcibly pulled him off. "Behave yourself, you imp," he snapped, and thrust him into Miranda's arms. "Wish us all Happy Christmas and say good night!"

But the boy, his trembling lips pressed firmly together and his eyes teary, would not say a word. He threw his father a look of heartfelt reproach and buried his face in his governess's shoulder. Miranda carried him up the stairs. The others either smiled in amusement or sighed in sympathy with the child as they wound their mufflers round their necks, drew on their gloves and started out to the sleigh. A young child exhibiting pique made a minor incident, requiring no further attention, they all believed. All except Barnaby.

Terence, ushering his guests out the door, noticed that his brother remained fixed in his place, peering up the stairway with knit brows. "Barnaby, old fellow, don't worry about Jamie. He'll cry himself to sleep and forget the whole thing by morning. Come along now. We're all waiting."

"Go without me, will you, Terence? I think I'd rather stay home tonight and . . . and read."

"Read?" Terence regarded his brother in puzzled disapproval. Reading was not a pastime the older man often engaged in, and he didn't understand its appeal. "Well, suit yourself," he said, shrugging, "though why anyone would wish to remain alone in the house on Christmas Eve with only a book for company is beyond my ken."

Barnaby waited until the sound of the sleigh bells died away. Then he went up the stairs two at a time. He found his nephew in his bedroom, sitting on Miranda's lap in a rocking chair near the window. Miranda was soothing the boy with soft, cooing words. "In a year or two," she was murmuring, "you'll be such a very big boy, quite old enough to—" She glanced up and saw Barnaby standing in the doorway. Her eyes at first gleamed with delight, but immediately afterward they became wary. "Look, Jamie, it's your uncle," she said, cocking her head curiously.

"Unca Barney!" the child clarioned, his tearful face brightening. "You didn't go!"

"No." Barnaby stepped over the threshold. "I stayed behind to be with you."

The boy jumped from Miranda's lap, ran across the room and clasped Barnaby's legs deliriously. "Did you thtay to tell me a thtory?"

Barnaby lifted him up in his arms. "Yes, if Mrs. Velacott will permit you to stay up just a wee bit longer."

"You'll thay yeth, won't you, Mithuth Velacott? Unca Barney tellth the betht thtorieth—Jack the Giant Killer . . . Thaint George an' the Dragon . . . King Arthur an' hith Knighth . . ."

"Of course I'll say yes," Miranda smiled, rising from the rocker, "if he doesn't tell all of them tonight."

Barnaby laughed. "I promise to tell only one," he said.

Miranda felt a little tremor in her chest. This usually sullen man so rarely smiled at her that the effect of his laugh was surprising—it warmed her through. "But Jamie," she said, trying not to be distracted from her responsibilities, "I think, first, you should get into your nightshirt."

The undressing was done with astounding dispatch. Then Barnaby sat down on the rocker with the child in his lap. Miranda started for the door. "Don't you want to thtay?" Jamie asked.

Miranda met Barnaby's eyes. "Oh, I don't think your uncle would like—"

"Do stay, Mrs. Velacott," Barnaby said, "unless you've something better to do."

"There'th nothing better than one of your thtorieth," the boy insisted.

"Then of course I *must* stay," Miranda agreed, and she perched on the edge of the boy's bed.

Jamie looked from one to the other happily. "Thith will be better than goin' to church. Go on, Unca Barney. Thtart."

Barnaby launched into an account of *The Marvelous*

Adventures of Sir Thomas Thumb, but before he'd concluded the second adventure, the child was fast asleep. Barnaby carried the boy to his bed and Miranda tucked the comforter around him. Then she blew out the candle, and they tiptoed from the room.

They walked together down the corridor. It was dimly lit by the candles in the wall sconces and quite chilly. Miranda pulled her shawl tightly round her shoulders. "It was good of you to stay," she said. "You made the boy's Christmas Eve a happy one."

"I enjoyed it myself. I remember too well what it was like being the youngest in a lively family. I like helping Jamie get through some of the torment." He threw Miranda an inscrutable look. "The boy seems to be growing quite attached to you."

"Yes, I think he is." They'd arrived at her door, but before going in, she peered at him curiously. "One would think you'd be pleased, sir, but something in your tone suggests otherwise."

He paused and faced her. "Why should I be pleased? I know quite well that you're only playing at being a governess. When the position bores you or becomes too onerous, you'll undoubtedly depart for something more entertaining, and the child will be left bereft."

A wave of irritation washed over her. "Dash it, Mr. Traherne, I'm tired of the groundless assumptions you make about me. You met me less than a week ago. What can you know of me to support the accusation that I am not serious about my post?"

"I know enough."

"Do you, indeed? And just what do you know?"

"I know, for one thing, that your identity is a lie. You are not Mrs. Velacott but *Lady* Velacott."

Her eyes fell guiltily. "Delia—Mrs. Traherne—told you, I suppose. If she did, then she also told you *why*—"

"She did *not* tell me. I knew it from the first."

She looked up at him again, her eyes flashing fire. "Now *you* are lying," she accused. "The first name you called me was Miss Pardew, not Lady Velacott."

"Nevertheless I knew. As I also know that you are reputed to have spent your youth in flirtations, to have devastated a number of men, and that you are more at home in ballrooms than in schoolrooms. In short, ma'am, hardly the sort suited to the care of children."

She felt choked with anger, not knowing how to argue against so closed a mind. "But this is all based on unsubstantiated rumors you must have heard more than a decade ago! How can you believe—?"

"I can believe them because they are *not* unsubstantiated. I myself can substantiate them."

"Are you saying you *knew* me in my youth?" She stared at him aghast, wondering which of her youthful excesses he'd observed that had evidently left such a dreadful impression on him. "But even if you did, what does it matter? It was all so long ago. Can you not grant the possibility that I'm changed?"

"Not so very changed," he said, his eyes measuring her from her face to the hands clutching her shawl over her revealing décolletage to the green shine of her gown which clung so enticingly to her breasts and hips and legs. Perhaps it was the gown, and the memories and feelings it invoked, that drove him to commit the final cruelty. His mouth curled upward in the disparaging sneer that had frightened away so many young women. "No, not so very changed. In fact, I heard you described quite recently as a baggage."

The blood drained from her face. *"Baggage?"* she croaked. White-lipped and trembling with rage, she wanted only to strike his cruel face. She swung up her hand to slap him, her shawl slipping unheeded from her shoulder. "You . . . you—!"

He caught her arm in midair. His blood began to bubble with an excitement he had no wish to control. With no real plan or intention in mind, he twisted her arm behind her and pulled her to him, feeling only a wicked pleasure in having her in his power, in being able to wreak a revenge for wounds that, he now realized, had never healed. Almost coldly, he took her chin in his free hand, tilted up her face and kissed her, the pressure of his lips hard and angry as a blow.

She struggled to free herself, striking his arm and shoulder with her free hand and twisting her head to wrench her mouth from his, but his grip was like a vise that only grew tighter with her resistance. After a while, she surrendered and lay limp in his hold.

From that moment, the nature of the embrace changed for him. As soon as she'd ceased her struggle, and he felt her softness against him, something melted in his chest. He lifted his head and eased the grip on her arm, his anger and lust for revenge somehow dissipated. He expected her to push him away, slap him, or scream, but she didn't move. She only peered at him with eyes wide and mouth slightly open, her lips trembling and her breath coming in gasps. *Let her go,* his mind told him. *Use your good sense and let her go.*

But he could not let her go. Acting purely on instinct, he let his hands move slowly up her arms, linger on her bare shoulders and then move to her throat, the throat that had so attracted him when he'd first laid eyes on her. He could feel the swelling curves of it under his fingers and the rapid, thrilling throb of her pulse underneath. He moved his hands to her chin and then, cupping her face with both hands, kissed her again, so tenderly that it elicited a soft moan from the depths of her.

The sound made him wild. His hands moved down again, quickly this time, and he took her in his arms, kissing her hungrily, with the starved passion of eleven years of waiting. But what surprised him more than his own impetuosity was her response. Her arms crept up around his neck, clutching him tightly, her lips clinging to his, as if she, too, had lost her head. He felt dizzy, shaken, more deeply stirred than he'd ever been by a woman's embrace. That realization horrified him. This was *Miranda Pardew,* the woman he despised!

Abruptly he pushed her away. She tottered back against

the wall, blinking at him, the picture of agonized confusion. Her eyes searched his face for some sort of explanation for what he knew was utterly crazed behavior.

But, furious with himself and as confused as she, he had no intention of attempting an explanation. He merely bent down, picked up her fallen shawl and thrust it at her. "I'm sorry," he muttered.

She used the shawl to wipe away a tear that had escaped from one of her startled, angry eyes. "You neither look nor sound sorry."

"Very well, then, I'm not sorry. Make of it what you will." And he turned on his heel and strode off down the corridor without a backward look.

· Seventeen ·

BARNABY WENT THROUGH the motions of Christmas Day, laughing and cavorting with his brothers and his nephews, playing Forfeits and Hunt the Slipper, drinking his share from the wassail bowl, and even making the dignified Lady Isabel giggle by kissing her ear under the mistletoe. But he did it all in a sort of fog. All day long, his mind played and replayed memories of the night before, like a simple tune one can't get out of one's head. Half distracted, he could still feel Miranda's lips on his mouth, the silken feel of her skin under his fingers, the softness of her body pressed against his. But the memories were not nostalgic; rather, they filled him with disgust. Disgust at his own weakness. Disgust at the realization that she still had the power to turn him into a blithering fool.

After an enormous Christmas dinner of goose and roast beef and smoking plum pudding and any number of other delicacies, the party divided into small groups and went off in separate directions: the children were taken wearily to bed; Lady Isabel and Harry strolled off with elaborate nonchalance to the small sitting room for a bit of lovers' privacy; Terence, Honoria, Lawrence and Livy sat down to a game of silver loo in the drawing room; and Delia set about helping the staff to clear the remains of the celebration and prepare for Boxing Day. That left Barnaby free to wander off by himself and try to clear his head. He went to the library, pulled a wing chair close to the fire and sat down to brood.

If this were a crisis in the Foreign Office, he told himself, he would know how to handle it. He would, first, clarify the nature of the problem. Then he'd list a number of alternate possibilities for a solution and evaluate them. Finally, after choosing the likeliest alternative, he'd proceed to get it done. This method was a useful, rational one, and, as far as he could tell, should work for personal problems as well as for professional ones.

Well then, he told himself, *let's get at it. What, exactly, is my problem?* But clarifying the problem was not easy. He mulled it over for several minutes, but the contradictory feelings that were tearing him apart—wild attraction and utter revulsion toward the same woman at the same time— were not easy to verbalize. The only honest statement he could contrive that clearly and accurately pinpointed the problem was: *I am falling in love with a woman I despise.* With this sentence, the illogic of his situation was immediately apparent. How could he find a logical solution for so ridiculous a problem?

It was obvious that the contrary feelings could not exist together; he had to rid himself of either the revulsion or the attraction. And since he'd lived with the revulsion for so long that it was now almost a part of him, it was the attraction that had to end. Separating himself from the source of that attraction seemed the easiest solution. Either Miranda had to leave this house, or he did. When he'd first learned that Miranda was to become governess in this house, he'd considered telling Delia what he thought of her, expecting that Delia would immediately sack the woman. But he hadn't done it. And now that Miranda was becoming a part of the household, and the boys were beginning to hold her in affection, it seemed a cruel thing to do. It would be easier on everyone if he simply took himself out of this house. All he had to do was invent an excuse for leaving and depart in the morning.

The plan was barely framing itself in his mind when the library door opened and Delia entered. She carefully closed it behind her, came up to the fire and seated herself on the hearth. "All right, my dear," she said, folding her hands in her lap and meeting his eyes with a level look in her own, "tell me what's troubling you?"

He shifted uncomfortably in his chair. "Why do you think anything's troubling me?"

"Come now, Barnaby, I've known you all your adult life. Do you think I can't tell when you're distracted?"

"I'm not distracted, exactly. Just . . . er . . . uncomfortable."

"Uncomfortable?"

"Yes, uncomfortable about telling you that I must cut my visit short."

Her eyebrows lifted in surprise. "How short?"

"I must go tomorrow."

"Good God! Why?" She peered at him worriedly. "Are you ill?"

"No, of course not. I simply must get home."

"But I don't understand. What must you do at home?"

"Er . . . nothing. Business."

She recognized evasion when she heard it. And her nature was too forthright to pretend she believed him. "What business can you have that came up so suddenly?" she asked bluntly. "You can't have had a message from London. No stage has yet come through."

He frowned, annoyed at himself for having launched on this course of lying without proper preparation. "It's something I knew about before I started." He looked down at his hands awkwardly. "I should have told you before, but I didn't wish to spoil the holiday."

"Barnaby, my boy, you are the worst liar in Christendom. I wish you would tell me the truth. I shan't hold you back if you truly must leave, but I'd feel much better knowing the real reason. It isn't something I've done or neglected to do, is it?"

"No, of course it isn't. Don't even *think* anything so

foolish. You know you've always made me feel perfectly at home."

"Then what *is* it? It isn't having to play the gallant to little Livy, is it? I warned Honoria that you might not like being compelled to court the girl."

"Compelled to court Livy? To *court* her?" Barnaby looked over at his sister-in-law in sincere surprise. "Is *that* why she's here? So that I can court her?"

"Why did you *think* she's here? Really, Barnaby, you are unbelievably naive when it comes to female wiles. Honoria has been trying to marry you off for years! And all the ladies in her circle have aided and abetted her in that attempt. In fact, little Livy was the unanimous choice of all of them."

"You don't say!" Barnaby grinned, more amused at this news than annoyed. "Whatever made them think that a young chit out of the schoolroom, with nothing to say for herself except how much she misses her mama, would catch my fancy?"

"She not a chit out of the schoolroom. She's twenty-two! And she's soft-spoken and modest, as you are, with a gentle disposition, proper rearing and, above all, very lovely to look at. Quite the perfect girl for you, wouldn't you say?"

Barnaby stared at his sister-in-law openmouthed, for a completely new solution to his problem burst upon him. *Livy Ponsonby*, gentle and modest and pretty as a picture! Why couldn't he make himself fall in love with *her*? The best way to get over one love was to find oneself another, he knew that. Another girl could be the perfect antidote to his heartache. That solution would be much better than making an awkward departure, better than enduring a lonely ride back to London through the cold and snow, better than tearing himself from the warmth of his family circle. "I wonder, Delia," he said thoughtfully, "if Honoria hasn't done me a favor. Perhaps courting Livy is just what I should do."

"What?" Delia asked, startled. "You don't intend to leave here after all?"

"No. On second thought, my business in London can wait."

"Can it, indeed?" She eyed him suspiciously. "You're cutting it too rare and thick, Barnaby Traherne. Just what is going on in that head of yours?"

"Nothing that need worry you. You've persuaded me that it is more important for me to learn the ways of females than to take care of business. I'm thirty years old, after all. It's time I did a little courting. And Livy Ponsonby *is* a sweet, pretty little thing, just as you said she is."

"I don't believe a word of this," Delia declared, rising majestically, "but as long as you're not going away, I shan't press you further. But be warned, my dear, I shall get to the bottom of this enigma sooner or later."

"There is no enigma," he insisted, rising also, "but if it amuses you to imagine there is, go ahead." He preceded her to the door and held it open for her. "By the way, Delia," he said casually, "Mrs. Velacott tells me you know her real identity. Is that true?"

Delia paused in the doorway. "That she's *Lady* Velacott, you mean? Yes, she told me all about it."

"Doesn't her misrepresentation trouble you?"

"No, of course not. Why should it?"

He shrugged. "I don't know, quite. But if I were hiring someone to look after my boys, I would be leery of someone who lied."

"She had good reason for dropping her title. The woman is penniless, you know. Her deceased husband left her without a farthing. As she quite sensibly explained to me, a title has no value to an impoverished female. So she dropped it. It's not really a lie, under the circumstances, is it?"

Barnaby peered at her for a moment, his expression strangely arrested. "No, I suppose not," he mumbled after a long pause.

Delia cocked her head at him, her shrewd eyes suddenly alight. "I say, Barnaby, that's the second time you've shown an undue interest in our governess. Is there some significance in these inquiries?"

"Don't make this part of your enigma, my love," he answered flippantly. "I already told you I don't like her above half."

"So you did. But you didn't tell me why."

He shrugged and started off down the corridor away from her. "She isn't my sort, that's all," he said over his shoulder.

"Not like little Livy, is that what you mean?" she called after him.

"No. Not a bit like little Livy."

Delia gazed after him, her eyes twinkling speculatively. "But at least our Mrs. Velacott can speak of more interesting things than missing her mama," she said under her breath. "And I have a feeling that you, Barnaby Traherne, are even more aware of that than I."

· *Eighteen* ·

MIRANDA STOOD AT the schoolroom window, looking down at the snowy landscape beneath her. But it was not the appeal of nature that had attracted her eye. It was the sight of two figures cavorting in the snow. Ever since Boxing Day, for three mornings in a row, Barnaby Traherne had taken Livy Ponsonby walking. Sometimes they strolled sedately arm in arm, but at other times, as now, they capered about like children, throwing snowballs at each other or tumbling about in the drifts. It was a sight Miranda found completely odious.

She turned away and fixed her eyes on her three charges, now bent over their slates, busily occupied with their lessons. A little while ago, she'd had to break up a fight (the usual tussle between Maury, who'd been teasing Jamie, and George, who'd charged in to defend his baby brother with clenched fists), but now all was calm. George was wrestling with a problem in long division, Maury with multiplication, and Jamie with listing "-AT" words—*b*at, *c*at, *h*at, and so on—laboriously on his slate. Their boyish absorption in their tasks made the governess smile. Each of them had an unconscious habit—a small gesture that revealed the intensity of his concentration: George pulled at his left earlobe, Maury twisted a lock of his hair, and as for Jamie, the tip of his tongue stuck out of the corner of his mouth and wiggled with every stroke of his chalk.

She walked slowly round the table looking over their shoulders, but none of her charges seemed, at the moment, to require her help. Then she wandered over to the bookshelf, looking for something to do, but the books were all neatly arranged. So, quite against her will, she found herself drawn back to the window and the view outside. The couple below were now chasing Miss Ponsonby's bonnet, which had blown off. As Miranda watched, Barnaby caught it and placed it back on the girl's head. The act was tenderly performed; he even tied the ribbons himself. For one horrible moment, Miranda feared he was going to lift the girl's chin and kiss her!

But he did not. He merely took her arm in his, and they strolled back toward the house.

Miranda sank down on the window seat, her heart beating rapidly and her emotions in turmoil. She couldn't understand why the scene below had such a powerful effect on her. Barnaby Traherne's doings were of no concern to her!

She couldn't help wondering, however, if he'd ever kissed Miss Ponsonby. But even if he had, it could not have been in the same way he'd kissed her. Miranda was not a green girl; she knew that the kiss they'd exchanged the other night was quite out of the ordinary. The memory of it still had the power to set her trembling.

The trouble was that she couldn't understand Barnaby Traherne's behavior. It was plain that he'd taken her in dislike, probably because he'd seen her in her youth indulging in some flagrant flirtation. That much was easy to fathom. But that abominable kiss had thrown everything askew. Perhaps he'd begun it as an act of dislike—more of an assault than a kiss, really—but he certainly hadn't ended it that way. She'd felt the tremor in his arms, the urgency in his embrace, the passion and hunger that had shaken them both. What had he meant by such an act? *Make of it what you will*, he'd said, but she couldn't make any sense of it at all.

She couldn't make much sense of her own feelings, either. Barnaby was sullen and insulting to her, yet, knowing this, she still was drawn to him. His way with Jamie endeared him to her, and she found his demeanor within his family circle warm and charming. The contradictions in her feelings were epitomized by her reactions to that kiss, at first so infuriating and later so . . . so overwhelming. At first, she'd wanted nothing more than to strike him down and stamp on his limp and prostrate body, but later, when he'd shown that unexpected tenderness and then such shattering passion, her whole body had responded. She would have clung to him forever, if he'd continued to hold her so.

But he hadn't continued. He'd made another of his abrupt mood changes. Cold and distant, he'd stalked away, leaving her shaken and confused. And shaken and confused she remained.

In the last analysis, however, the matter was not so confusing. If one faced it honestly, it was quite simple. She could state the problem in fewer than ten words: *I'm in love with a man who despises me.*

And now he was pursuing Livy Ponsonby. Surely he couldn't be serious. His character was too complex and too subtle to find the naive Livy interesting. Yet, on second thought, Miranda couldn't blame him for taking her up. Livy, besides being a beauty, had the more significant advantage of being quiet, sweet and virtuous. She was not wasting her youth in wild behavior and meaningless flirtations. Barnaby would not be able to accuse *her* of being a liar and a flirt.

Very well, she said, addressing him in her mind, *if that's the sort of namby-pamby female who pleases you, I wish you well of her. Go ahead and woo her, with my blessing.*

Miranda peered out of the window again, but the two of them were gone. There was nothing to see now but the impressions of their movements in the snow. Footprints, male and female, side by side. The molded remains of a scene of blossoming romance. How picturesque. How romantic. How utterly revolting.

· Nineteen ·

DELIA, COMING CHEERFULLY down the stairs after a very satisfactory visit to the schoolroom (during which George cogently explained to her the causes of the War of the Roses, Maury exhibited a proud proficiency in multiplying double digits, and Jamie wrote half the alphabet for her in capital letters on his slate), was startled to discover her dignified sister-in-law, Honoria, down on one knee outside the closed library door, her eye to the keyhole. "Heavens, Honoria," she exclaimed, "are you *eavesdropping*?"

"Sssh!" Honoria hissed, waving a hand at her in a gesture of restraint and not even bothering to look up. "I think he's going to *offer* for her!"

"Who? *Barnaby?*" Delia hurried to the doorway, her cheery mood dissipating. "Good God! You don't mean it!"

"Hush, I said! Do you want them to hear us?" Honoria tottered to her feet and drew Delia down the hall so they would be out of hearing of the pair inside the library. "I'm so excited I can hardly *breathe*!"

"Why?" Delia asked suspiciously, not wanting to be taken in by Honoria's histrionic fervor. "What makes you think—?"

Honoria clasped her hands at her breast, her eyes shining. "He's taken her in there, just the two of them," she whispered gleefully, "and he's teaching her to play *Hearts*!"

"Well, what of that? There's nothing especially meaningful in two people playing a simple card game."

"Yes, but I don't remember Barnaby ever doing such a thing before. And there's something about him today. Something edgy. Why, at breakfast this morning, he dropped the jam jar."

"Then that settles it," Delia said dryly. "Dropping the jam jar is all the proof one needs."

That remark did succeed in deflating Honoria's high spirits. Her smile transformed itself into a glare. "What sort of proof do you need, for heaven's sake?" she retorted. "It's as plain as pikestaff he's pursuing her."

"If you'd seen through the keyhole that he was down on his knee before her, I might have taken you seriously. But frankly, Honoria, I don't believe he can be such a fool as that."

Honoria's whole body stiffened. "Why, whatever can you mean? Don't you *want* him to marry?"

"Yes, of course I do. But not your little Livy."

"Why not? What's wrong with her?"

"Nothing's wrong with her. But nothing's right with her, either."

"*Everything*'s right with her!" Honoria exclaimed, ready to defend the girl to the death. Having convinced herself that Livy was the ideal partner for her dearest Barnaby, she would not give up that dream merely on Delia's say-so. "She's well-bred and pretty and kind and shy . . ."

Delia expelled a grunt of disgust. "I don't know why you think Barnaby needs a shy, retiring flower of a female."

"Because he's so shy himself," Honoria declared without hesitation. It was the same argument she'd used with her friends in London, so it came easily to her tongue. "He's not attracted to those over-animated, domineering sorts."

"Barnaby is *not* shy, Honoria. You must stop believing that he is. He hasn't been shy since early manhood. And an animated woman is probably the only sort who'll keep him interested."

Honoria blinked at her younger sister-in-law, her confidence shaken. "How can you sound so sure, Delia? Has he said anything to you on the subject?"

"No, not much. But I have good instincts in these matters. And my instincts tell me that he'd grow bored with the likes of Livy Ponsonby in a very short time. I think he'd do much better with someone like . . . well, like my governess."

"Your *governess*!" Honoria eyes popped, her face reddened, and her voice rose to a squeak. "Your governess would be the very *worst* choice for him. Do you know who she *is*?"

"What sort of question is that? Of course I know who she is. She's Mrs. Velacott. Or *Lady* Velacott, if her dropped title is what's bothering you."

"That's *not* what's bothering me. She's *Miranda Pardew*!"

"Heavens," Delia said, puzzled. "You say that as if you were saying Lucrezia Borgia. Who's Miranda Pardew?"

"Miranda Pardew, I'll have you know," Honoria ranted, "is the woman who made mincemeat of poor Barnaby at his very first ball. I blame her, and her alone, for his avoidance of females and for his bleak and miserable bachelor existence."

Delia stared at her sister-in-law, her breath arrested in her throat. "Good God," she gasped after a moment, "is that *true*? My governess is the same woman who offended Barnaby all those years ago?"

"As true as I'm standing here. She is one woman, believe me, whom I shall never forget!"

"Aha," Delia crowed as if in triumph, "I *thought* there was something havey-cavey about his interest in her."

"See here, Delia Traherne, if you're speaking of Barnaby, you can be certain that he *has* no interest in her! The woman is nothing but a . . . a . . . *flibbertigibbet*."

"She may well have been, for all I know," Delia acknowledged. "But it was long ago, wasn't it? Even Lucrezia Borgia turned out to be praiseworthy in the latter part of her life."

"What has Lucrezia Borgia to do with this?" Honoria snapped disgustedly.

"Never mind." Delia eyed Honoria with a speculative gleam. "When, exactly, did this infamous set-down business occur?"

"I don't remember *exactly* when. Ten or eleven years ago. Barnaby was nineteen."

"And he remembers the incident, I suppose."

"All too well. He recognized her at once. She, of course, has no recollection of the incident or the devastation she caused, the heartless creature."

"I shouldn't think she would. One can't be expected to remember *all* the foolish acts of one's youth." Delia rubbed her chin thoughtfully for a moment, and then, as a wicked smile suffused her face, she grasped her sister-in-law's arm. "Honoria, my love, come with me into the sitting room. I'll have Cummings bring us some soothing tea, we'll put our feet up, and you'll tell me every detail of this fascinating story."

Honoria, although quite suspicious and full of objections to everything Delia said and was not saying, allowed herself be led away. "I don't understand you, Delia. Why on earth do you wish to hear those unpleasant details?"

"Because I'm beginning to understand the enigma of Barnaby's heart. I think, my dear, that we may have stumbled upon the one woman who'd be a perfect match for our Barnaby. With a bit of good fortune, we may marry him off after all." She squeezed Honoria's arm affectionately before giving a final blow to her sister-in-law's hopes. "But *not*," she added, laughing, "to your little Livy."

· *Twenty* ·

IN THE LIBRARY, completely unaware of the scheming going on in his behalf right outside the door, Barnaby sat at a small card table in front of one of the windows dealing cards to Livy Ponsonby, who sat opposite him. They'd been playing long enough for him to realize that Livy did not play cards with the same zest for winning that Miranda had exhibited when he'd played with her at the inn. At that time, he'd found Miranda's chortling triumph quite annoying, but he now reluctantly recognized that her enthusiasm had added to the game a vivacity that was absent here, with Livy showing such good-natured indifference to the outcome. "Are you sure you'd enjoy playing another rubber?" he asked, searching her face for signs of boredom.

She threw him one of her sweet, sincere smiles. "Yes, of course," she said. "Positively."

The game proceeded quietly, the only sounds being the occasional snap of sparks from the fireplace and the occasional groan from Barnaby when his luck was bad. Livy didn't say a word. Barnaby glanced up at her from time to time, wondering what the girl was thinking. Was it wise, he wondered, to pursue a girl who never made her thoughts or feelings known?

Playing Hearts with Livy did not occupy his full attention, so his mind roamed about at will. This afternoon he was preoccupied with the question of offering for her. Honoria had hinted quite broadly at breakfast that she was expecting to hear the happy news within the next few days. Honoria was right about the importance of prompt action. If he truly intended to offer for the girl, he ought to do it soon. There were only a few days left before this fortnight's visit came to an end. The matter would have to be broached before Lawrence and Honoria took Livy back to her mama. Positively.

But somehow he couldn't seem to bring himself to the sticking point. Although he was sincerely taken with the girl—she had a lovely face and form, a most pleasing voice, the modest demeanor that he believed enhanced a woman's appeal and, at times, a look in her large, shockingly blue eyes of surprised fright that never failed to touch him and make him feel protective toward her—he felt, in her company, that something important was missing. The trouble was that he couldn't figure out what that something was.

As these thoughts were circling round in his mind, the library door opened and Miranda came in, heading for the bookcases. A moment passed before she saw them. When she did, she stopped dead in her tracks. Her cheeks reddened painfully. "I'm so sorry!" she gasped. "I didn't know—"

Barnaby peered at her in some surprise. He had not seen her since Christmas Eve, when she was wearing her green gown and her hair was gloriously tumbled about her face. She was now wearing her blue muslin with the white ruffle, and her hair was covered with her widow's cap. She hardly looked like the strumpet he'd conjured up in his memory. "That's quite all right," he assured her politely. "You are only interrupting a card game. Livy, my dear, it was Mrs. Velacott who taught me to play this game."

"Did she really?" Livy gave the governess a warm smile.

"Yes, I did," Miranda said, speaking rapidly to mask her embarrassment. "I'm glad to discover, Mr. Traherne, that you still remember it. But let me not interrupt." She backed awkwardly to the door. "I'll come back later."

"That's not necessary," Barnaby said, rising. "Please do what you came to do."

As she hesitated in the doorway, he stared at her with what he knew was undue intensity. He'd scrupulously avoided her since Christmas Eve, five whole days ago. When he wanted to see his nephews—which he liked to do daily—he sent the butler up to get them. Miranda tactfully had not accompanied them on those occasions. Now he could not tear his eyes away. It was as if they'd been starved for the sight of her. But this sort of thinking, he knew, was contrary to the rules he'd set for himself. Such thoughts were dangerous. "Were you looking for something, ma'am?" he asked, his tone formal and distant.

"Yes," she said, stepping back into the room. "The last volume of Smollett's *History*. We took only three volumes upstairs the other day, but today I learned there are four."

"There are indeed. Come in, ma'am, please. I'll help you search for it."

Before she could object, he crossed to the shelves nearest the window and began to look. She went to the opposite side. Since the books were shelved in no discernable order, it was necessary to read the title of each one. Many minutes passed in silence. Finally, squatting down and peering through the tomes on the lowest shelf, Barnaby came upon it. "Here it is, sandwiched between John Wesley's *Primitive Physic* and Madame D'Arblay's *Journal*," he announced.

Miranda ran quickly to his side to get it, arriving and bending down for it just as he was rising. He didn't see her, for though the Smollett's was in his hand, his eyes were still on the other books on the shelf. The top of his head struck her chin with a loud clunk. She cried out and tottered back. "Damnation!" he swore, dropping the book and reaching for her with quick instinct to keep her from falling over. "I'm so sorry!" he muttered. "Are you hurt?"

But before the words had left his lips, he realized he was holding her round the waist. For a fraction of a second their eyes met. Then he dropped his hold on her with the alacrity with which one drops a hot coal.

"N-No, don't b-be alarmed," she stammered. "I'm all right."

He nodded and handed her the book. She took it, made a quick curtsey and fled from the room.

"I don't think she was hurt," Livy said calmly from her place at the card table.

He looked round in surprise. He'd forgotten she was there. Embarrassed, and with his feelings in turmoil, he returned to the card table. "Where were we?" he asked absently.

"Perhaps we ought to start this game again," she suggested, her manner so placid and sweet that it was obvious she'd seen nothing untoward in what had just passed.

He fixed his eyes on her as his racing pulse quieted itself. There was something soothing in Livy's company. Being wedded to her would be calm and reasonable and eminently sane. He would never feel the turmoil, the tension, the downright agony that he invariably experienced when Miranda was anywhere near. He needed protection against the disquieting feelings that Miranda always generated. Livy could be that protection. If he had a brain in his head, he would propose marriage to this girl. Right now.

Livy looked across at him with her big blue eyes. "Is it my turn to deal?"

"Your turn? Yes, I believe it is your turn. Livy, my sweet, will you marry me?"

It was done. Said and done. His chest heaved with a large, relieved breath. He smiled over at the girl for whom he'd just offered, confident that he'd made both of them very happy.

But Livy, her mouth slightly open, was staring at him with her shocked, fearful, helpless look. "Wh-what did you s-say?" she asked.

"I'm sorry, my dear," he said contritely, realizing that he'd not shown an iota of romance in his proposal. "I was thoughtlessly abrupt. But you must have known what my intentions were. Surely I've shown you how much I care for you. I'm asking you to marry me."

Her eyes opened even wider. "Oh!" she breathed. Her response was unquestionably more frightened than happy.

He reached for her hand. "May I take that as a 'yes'?"

The little hand trembled under his, and her eyes fell from his face, her long lashes brushing her cheeks. They sat, silent and unmoving, for a long moment. Then she wriggled her hand free, stood up and looked down at him. "Yes," she breathed. "Th-thank you."

"Do you mean it?" he asked, getting to his feet and smiling down at her. "Positively?"

She didn't laugh, nor did she meet his eyes. She merely nodded. "M-Mama will be so g-glad," she said, and then she, too, fled from the room.

Barnaby gazed after her in bewilderment. For the second time in less than five minutes, a woman had fled from him. "Barnaby, my boy," he muttered dryly under his breath, "how do you account for this magical effect you have on the ladies?"

· Twenty-one ·

BARNABY, UNCERTAIN OF the meaning of Livy's response, said nothing to anyone that afternoon about being betrothed. And Livy, hiding away in her room, had neither the opportunity nor the inclination to make any announcement. But in the mysterious way that such news has of disseminating itself, the whole household was buzzing with it within an hour. Honoria heard about it from her abigail when the girl was brushing her hair, preparing to dress it for dinner. Honoria let out a little scream. "How did you *hear* it?" she cried, clasping her hands together at her breast. "Are you *sure*?"

"Everyone's whisperin' about it," the girl said. "Even Mr. Cummings won't deny it, an' he ain't one to permit us t' spread gossip."

That was enough for Honoria. Pulling her dressing gown tightly around her ungirdled waist, and with her long gray hair hanging unplaited down her back, she ran first to the Earl to tell him the news and then down the hall to Barnaby's room. "Dearest!" she exclaimed as soon as he opened his door, "I'm so delighted I could weep!" And she threw herself into his arms.

He patted her affectionately on her back as he led her to the nearest chair. "Calm yourself, my dear," he warned. "I'm not yet certain that Livy is happy about this."

"Of *course* she's happy. How can you think otherwise? Why, she told me herself that she finds you the kindest, most good-natured and handsomest man alive!"

Barnaby was not taken in by his sister-in-law's hyperbole. "I suspect, my love, that it was you put those words in her mouth. Nevertheless, you must promise me not to say a word of this betrothal until Livy herself affirms it."

Livy did affirm it that very evening at dinner. She made a shy announcement during the serving of the second course. And when the whole family reacted with boisterous delight (rising to their feet, surrounding the pair, pounding Barnaby on his back, kissing the blushing Livy and loudly toasting the couple's health), Barnaby was relieved to see that Livy did at last look happy.

A short while later, upstairs in the schoolroom, Miranda sat on the window seat staring out at a pale winter moon. The boys were not there, having been invited to join in the celebration of their uncle's betrothal, but Miranda had declined to go with them. "It's a celebration for the family," she'd explained as she sent them off in the care of the butler, "not for the staff."

She remained in the schoolroom alone, not noticing that the fire had died. She'd not even lit a candle to dispel the darkness. She merely sat gazing out at the sky. It was a sad-looking moon, she thought, coldly bluish white in color and fuzzy in outline because of a layer of clouds that partially obscured it. It barely gave light to the snow. *Pathetic*, she muttered. *Like me.*

Indeed, she *was* pathetic, sitting there in the corner of the window recess with her feet curled up under her and her arms crossed over her chest, shivering with cold and letting a veritable flood of tears drip down her cheeks. It was pathetic to weep over the betrothal of a man who had shown his dislike of her from the first moment they'd met. How could she have been so foolish as to permit herself to fall in love with him? Anyone with a grain of sense could have foretold that she would end up in tears.

She'd not used good sense in this matter. She'd let a kiss blind her to the facts. Barnaby Traherne had kissed her, and she'd made herself believe it was a meaningful act. But evidently it had meant nothing to him, for he was now betrothed to the insipid Miss Ponsonby. Of course, if Miss Ponsonby's kisses had the power to drive the memory of that other, extraordinary kiss from his mind, perhaps "little Livy" was not as insipid as she seemed!

Miranda tried to stop weeping by turning her mind to other matters, like her future. But how bleak her future suddenly appeared to be. Her prospects now seemed to have turned as cold and unexciting as that fuzzy moon. Thinking about Barnaby had given her days a little spice, the stimulus that comes from speculation. Each day a sense of expectation—the possibility of surprise—hovered in the air. With Barnaby lurking about to watch her handling of Jamie, to criticize her, to assault her in the corridor, there had been a zest to her days. Now that zest was gone, and nothing seemed likely to take its place. All she could look forward to now was his leaving. When he was gone, she could set her mind on forgetting him. The rest of the days of her life might not be eventful, but they might eventually be free of pain. That, at least, was something to look forward to.

And there was always memory. She could, in future, content herself with reviewing her few happy memories, as she used to do when her husband's behavior was at its worst. She used to finger her little cameo and remember that happiest month in her life when they were traveling on honeymoon in Italy. A pathetic kind of consolation, admittedly, but better than nothing.

Instinctively she uncrossed her arms, her fingers feeling for the cameo that had always hung round her neck on a silver chain. Nothing was there. She'd forgotten—the highwaymen had taken it. Even that innocuous solace was denied her.

A fresh flood of tears was about to flow when a knock at the door stopped them. Miranda brushed her cheeks free of wetness. "Come in," she said hoarsely.

"Miranda?" The door opened. Delia, her face eerily lit by the candle she carried, peered into the darkness. "Are you here?"

Miranda unfolded herself from the seat. "Yes, here I am."

Delia stepped over the threshold. "What are you doing sitting in the dark?" She went to the bookcase, took down another candle from the top shelf and lit it with her own.

Miranda blinked in the sudden light. "I was only . . . looking out at the moon. Did you wish to see me?"

"Yes. Miranda, my dear, why didn't you come down when we sent for you?"

"I'm sorry. I thought it was a family affair."

"Yes, so the boys explained." Delia set the two candles on the low schoolroom table and sat down at it. "But you must have understood that we wanted to include you."

Miranda did not answer. She remained standing in the shadows, trying to compose herself.

"I am not scolding," Delia assured her, looking over at the shadowy figure with a knit brow. "Was there any reason why you decided to stay up here alone?"

"I only . . . I thought . . . that is, if I may be honest, Delia, Mr. Barnaby Traherne has no liking for me. My presence at his celebration would not have added to his pleasure."

Delia did not deny the truth of that. "Do you know *why* Barnaby has no liking for you?" she asked in her forthright style.

"No, not really. But one doesn't have to have reasons for taking someone in dislike. Sometimes it's purely instinctive. I don't much like him, either."

"Don't you?" She cocked her head, trying to get a better look at Miranda's face, but the light of two candles was not enough to penetrate the shadows. "Do sit down, Miranda. You seem like a ghost standing there before the window, with the moonlight outlining you with eerie light."

Miranda laughed mirthlessly and came forward. "Shouldn't you be downstairs?" she asked as she sat down on one of the low chairs.

"I won't stay long enough to be missed." She looked across the table at the younger woman, noting the red-rimmed eyes. She believed she knew why Miranda had been crying. "You're wrong about Barnaby, you know," she said bluntly.

"Wrong? In what way?"

"In what you just said—that his dislike of you is instinctive. That dislike has nothing to do with instinct. I've learned he has quite specific reasons for his dislike."

Miranda immediately stiffened. "If you are referring to his disagreements with me about handling Jamie," she said defensively, "I believe those differences have been settled. Besides, he disliked me long before that."

"Yes, he did. Since his nineteenth year, I'm told."

"What?" Miranda's eyebrows rose in astonishment. "What on earth are you talking about? You know we met on the stagecoach, less than a fortnight ago."

"No. That's not so. I'm told you met at the Lydell ball eleven years ago."

"The Lydell ball? Eleven *years*—?" She gaped at Delia openmouthed, the words not making sense. She did have a vague memory of a ball at the Lydells' during the season before her betrothal. And, yes, she did remember that Rodney was there, and Fred Covington and Lord Yarmouth and a few other of her swains. But she had no recollection of Barnaby, not the slightest. "I would have remembered," she muttered, blinking into the candle flame in an effort to bring it all back. "A man like Barnaby, tall and handsome and distinguished . . . I would have remembered . . ."

"He was scarcely distinguished," Delia said gently. "Not at nineteen."

"No, I suppose not . . . but even so . . ."

"It was his first ball, Honoria tells me. He was gawky, and very shy."

Hearing those words, something flashed into Miranda's memory: she recalled standing on a sort of platform . . . a circle of admirers milling about . . . Rodney whispering the most charming of pleasantries into her ear . . . then, an interruption . . . the Earl of Shallcross—Yes! Lawrence Traherne, the very Earl now staying in this house!— thrusting a gawky, clumsy fool at her; a stuttering, ill-clad *fool* with a bad haircut . . . Oh, God! Was that *Barnaby*? Whom she teased and tormented and tossed aside, just to impress Rodney with her power over men!

"No," she groaned at this vision of her younger self, "*no!*" And she dropped her head in her arms on the table in shame.

"So you *do* remember the incident," Delia said.

"Yes, I remember. Now I remember. Oh, Delia, I could *die*!"

"That would be a rather severe punishment for the crime, wouldn't it?"

"No!" came the muffled cry from the buried head.

"Come now, Miranda," Delia scoffed, "it was a set-down, not a murder."

Miranda lifted her head. "It was the sorriest, most fla-grant example of arrogant vanity imaginable! If you had been there, you'd have hated me."

"Nonsense. And what difference does it make that I might have disliked you then? You are obviously not the same person. I like you *now*. Give yourself credit for having improved your character."

"No, I can't take credit. The trials of life improved my character, not I."

Delia pushed back her chair and rose. "If you're deter-mined to flagellate yourself over your long-past depravity, Miranda Velacott, I'm not going to stay here and watch you do it." She picked up one of the candles and started toward the door. "Good night, my dear."

"But Delia, wait! If it was not to berate me for that depravity, why did you tell me this now?"

Delia, her hand on the doorknob, turned a level gaze on the woman slumped over the table. "Because I wanted you to see on how slight a basis Barnaby built his dis-like."

"Slight?" Miranda sat erect in stern objection to Delia's belittlement of her crime. "It's not slight at all! What I did was unforgiveable."

"Heavens, woman, you sound as nonsensical as Honoria. You struck him with words, not sticks and stones."

Miranda shook her head. "Contempt can sometimes be more brutal than physical injuries, isn't that so?"

"Sometimes, perhaps, but in this case, contempt may be too strong a word. It seems to me—and I made this point to Honoria as strongly as I could—that the entire incident has been overblown. Much too overblown. And for far too long."

"Whether overblown or not, Delia, I suppose it's foolish to worry about it at this late date," Miranda sighed. She stood up, turned to the window and gazed out at the bleak, eerily lit landscape. "It cannot matter to Barnaby now. Not any more."

"If you think that," Delia remarked as she threw open the door and strode out of the room, "you're not nearly as astute a young woman as I think you are."

Miranda wheeled about. "Delia? What do you mean by that?" She ran across the room to the doorway. "Are you suggesting that he—? That I—? *Delia!*"

But the corridor was deserted. Delia was gone.

· Twenty-two ·

IT WAS MUCH later than his usual bedtime when the nursemaid undressed Jamie and tucked him in. But the boy was not sleepy. He lay awake waiting for someone to come in and give him a good-night embrace. Usually his mother did it, and sometimes Mrs. Velacott, but when he was really lucky, it was both. His mother's embrace was the best, of course, but Mrs. Velacott rated a close second. He could tell that the new governess really liked him, and that gave him a warm feeling inside. Besides, she had soft hands, softer even than Mama's, and the smoothest cheeks, and she always smelled like cinnamon candy. He wished that she or Mama would come. It was hard to fall asleep without a hug.

Tonight, however, a long time passed and no one came. He got up from his bed, wrapped his comforter around him to protect him from the cold and, after feeling his way to the door (for he was not permitted to light a candle on his own), went out the door and down the corridor to the schoolroom.

The room was very dimly lit by a guttering candle on the table, but he could see someone sitting on the window seat. "Mithuth Velacott?" he asked.

She turned round in surprise, wiping her cheek with the back of her hand. "J-Jamie? Why are you still awake?"

He waddled over to her, his comforter dragging behind him. "You didn't come to thay good night."

"Oh, that's right. I'm sorry. Come, give me your hand and I'll tuck you in properly."

He came closer and peered at her. "Were you crying, ma'am?"

"No, of course n—" She paused and thought better of her answer. "Well, yes, I was."

"Why?"

"Because I . . . I . . ." She looked down at his worried little face. His child-like affection touched her heart. "No good reason, really," she said, kneeling down and wrapping his comforter closely round his neck. "I was missing my . . . my cameo, that's all."

"What'th a cameo?"

"It's only a little trifle I used to wear round my neck."

The boy thought the answer strange. Why would one cry over a trifle? Unless . . . "Wath it like a good luck charm?" he asked.

"Yes, exactly like a good luck charm," she said, smiling at him proudly. "You are very understanding." She rose and took his hand.

"Did you mithplathe it? I can thtay and help you find it. I'm not a bit thleepy."

"I didn't misplace it, though I thank you for your offer to help."

"Then what happened to it?" he persisted as she led him from the room.

They went hand in hand down the corridor. "The highwaymen—the ones your uncle Barney told you about—they took it," she explained. "I'm afraid it's gone for good."

"That'th a shame," he said. "Unlucky."

The boy's concern for his governess's luck lasted all night and into the next day. It was a windy, overcast day, not conducive to outdoor games, so he and his brothers were forced to play indoors during what Mrs. Velacott called their morning "recess," an hour of unsupervised play. That was when Jamie told them about Mrs. Velacott's loss.

"Wouldn't it be thplendid if we could find the highwaymen?" he asked, his eyes shining.

"Splendid," Maury said in sarcastic agreement. "Except how would we find them?"

"It might not be too hard," George said thoughtfully. "The coach was attacked a few miles south of Wymondham. The thieves must have a hideaway somewhere nearby."

"Yeth!" the little fellow said excitedly. "We'd find 'em thouth of Wymondham. And then we could fight 'em an' thlit their throatth and get her lucky piethe back for her!"

"Yes, slit their throats! Good!" George smiled with pleasure, imagining the bloody scene. "We could fight them with our swords and demand their loot before hacking them to bits."

"Righto!" laughed Maury, pulling out his toy sword and flourishing it in the air before lunging at his older brother. "Take that, you varlet! Mrs. Velacott's cameo or your life!"

The boys skirmished about, brandishing their swords and making drama of the imagined confrontation. Jamie watched, wide-eyed. "Let'th do it!" he cried when both boys fell down on the floor, exhausted.

"Do what?" George asked.

"Fight the highwaymen with our thwordth and get the good luck piethe back."

"We just did," Maury said.

"No! For *real*!"

George got up and patted his little brother's head. "We will, Jamie, someday. When we're older," he said kindly.

"When? Thoon?"

George shrugged. "Next month."

Maury laughed, but Jamie took him seriously. "Nextht month? Do you promith? All three of uth?"

"No, you're too little," Maury teased. "George and I will fight the highwaymen, and when we bring back the cameo, you can give it to Mrs. Velacott and take all the credit."

Jamie glared at him. "It'th alwayth you and George. You never let me do anything mythelf."

"That's enough, Jamie. Don't start whining," George said, dismissing the subject. "Come on, Maury, let's play spillikins."

But Jamie wouldn't let it go. "I don't care what you do! Getting the good luck back wath *my* idea! I'll do it mythelf, thee if I don't!" And he stomped out of the room.

An hour later, when their lessons were resumed, Miranda asked where the child had gone. "Sulking in his room, probably," George said.

But he was not in his room. Miranda, after searching through every room on the third floor, grew alarmed. She sent the two older boys to seek out all the child's favorite haunts in the house, but they couldn't find him. "I'd wager the little bufflehead has gone looking for the highwaymen," Maury told the governess in disgust.

"The highwaymen? What do you mean?"

"He wants to be a hero and bring you back your missing cameo," George explained.

Miranda paled. "Do you mean to suggest he might have gone *outside*?"

George was not at all perturbed. "There's no need to fall into a taking, ma'am," he said reassuringly. "Jamie knows the way to the road. And the direction to Wymondham. When his feet get cold, he'll turn round and come home; you have my word."

But Miranda could not be so complacent. She set the two boys to their schoolwork, ran to her room for her cloak and bonnet and flew down the back stairs and out the kitchen door, making for the road. She was beside herself with alarm. Jamie had as much as a two-hour start. Even if she ran the entire three miles to Wymondham, she might not catch up with him. And if the child had got that far, there was no way of knowing where he might go from there.

She felt almost hysterical as she slogged through the snow toward the road, tying the ribbons of her bonnet as she stumbled along. The brim of her bonnet hid the sight of a man who was approaching, and she blundered into him. "Oh!" she gasped, startled.

"Damnation, woman, watch where you go!" came Barnaby's irritated voice.

She glanced up at him. "I beg your pardon," she said hastily, trying to pass him without further conversation.

He noticed her perturbation. "Wait a moment, ma'am," he ordered, holding her by the arms, his eyes searching her face. "What's amiss?"

"I must go!" She tried to shake off his hold. "Jamie's run off."

"Jamie?" He frowned down at her. "Don't be foolish. He wouldn't do such a thing."

"Please, let me go! I haven't time to explain. He's had a two-hour start. He may be more than halfway to Wymondham by this time."

"If this is true, ma'am, then there's a better way to catch up with him than shank's mare. Come with me to the stable. We'll take the sleigh."

A little while later, they were gliding swiftly along the road behind a pair of frisky horses, Barnaby holding the reins and Miranda peering anxiously at the passing landscape for a sign of Jamie's red knit cap and blue muffler. "It's all my fault," she moaned after a quarter-hour had passed with no sign of the child. "I told him about my cameo. He thinks it's my lucky piece. He's gone to find the highwaymen and get it back for me."

Barnaby grinned. "Good for him. Plucky little chap."

"How can you smile?" Miranda demanded. "What if we don't find him?"

"We'll find him. He's bound to follow the road."

"We can't be certain of that."

"No, but it's likely. He'd find the road easier going than the fields."

"But if he's already made it to Wymondham—"

"He hasn't. His legs are too short to make such good time. I doubt if he's much further along than— Wait! Look there! What's that ahead?"

She saw only a blur at first, but there was something red in it. As they drew closer, they could make him out. He was trudging along with weary determination, his muffler blowing out behind him and a toy sword hanging from a belt strapped about his waist.

"Oh, thank God!" Miranda whispered hoarsely.

Barnaby slowed the horses, and she leaped from the sleigh and ran to the child. "*Jamie*," she cried, kneeling beside him and embracing him, "you naughty imp! How *could* you frighten me so?"

"Mithuth Velacott!" His face lit up with joyful relief. "Have you come to take me home?"

"Yes, of course we've come to take you home. Your uncle Barney's brought the sleigh."

"I'm tho glad. My feet are *frothen*."

"I'm sure they are. Come along, then. We have a lap robe in the sleigh."

He took her hand. "I haven't yet got your good luck piethe back," he said, shamefaced.

"Don't trouble yourself about it," she said as she helped him up to the seat. "Finding you is all the good luck I need for one day."

They bundled him up in the lap robe. "I hope, Jamie, that you won't play such a trick as this again," his uncle lectured sternly. "You're not yet old enough to travel about on these roads alone."

"But I had to find the highwaymen, you thee," the child explained.

"No, you had not! Finding the highwaymen is my job."

"Yourth? Why?"

"Because it was I who was attacked by them. I want to fight my own battles, just as you want to fight yours."

The child looked up at his uncle adoringly. "*Are* you going to fight the highwaymen, then?"

"Yes, I am."

"And you'll bring Mithuth Velacott'th good luck piethe back to her?"

"Yes, I will."

"Will you mind, Mithuth Velacott, if Unca Barney geth your cameo inthtead of me?"

Barnaby looked over at her. "Will you mind, ma'am?"

Miranda, feeling her color rise, dropped her eyes. "I won't mind," she said to the boy.

Jamie snuggled up against his uncle contentedly. "Good, then, Unca Barney," he said, "I'll leave it to you." Snug and warm, and with his heavy responsibility lifted from his shoulders, he promptly fell asleep.

Barnaby held the horses to a relaxed pace. Now that the boy was found, there was no reason to hurry. Miranda threw a sidelong glance at him. "I hope, Mr. Traherne, that you don't really believe I was serious about the cameo. I would not wish you to do battle with the highwaymen for any reason at all, much less for the sake of such a trifle."

"My battle with the highwaymen will not be over a trifle," he assured her.

"That isn't the response I wished for," she said, frowning.

"You wished I'd say there would not be a battle at all, is that it?"

"Yes. The matter of the highwaymen is best forgotten."

"That, ma'am, is too womanish a point of view. For a man, it is not 'best' to forget when one has been robbed and assaulted."

"You must have vengeance, is that it?"

"I'd prefer to think of it as righting a wrong."

She looked over at him, taking in the manly grace of his posture, the relaxed ease of his hands on the reins, the breadth of his shoulders under the capes of his greatcoat, the strength of his profile under his high beaver hat. "You've changed a great deal since the Lydell ball," she said on a sudden impulse.

His head came round abruptly, his eyes ablaze with surprise and anger. She met his gaze without wavering. After a moment, he turned back to the horses. "I've not changed as much as you think," he said carefully. "I like to believe that, even at nineteen, I was not lacking in courage. I would have wanted to do battle with the highwaymen even then."

"Yes, I suppose you would." She lowered her eyes to the hands folded in her lap. "But in those days, I wouldn't have recognized courage," she admitted. "Not courage, nor sensitivity, nor true manliness, nor any worthwhile quality. I was a very poor judge of character back then—a silly chit, unable to see clearly."

He threw her a quick, questioning glance, wondering if he'd fully understood what she'd just said. Was she actually *apologizing* to him for what happened at the ball? And how was it that she so suddenly remembered an incident that she'd not had an inkling of a few days before? "What do you mean," he asked, temporizing to give himself time to think, "when you say you were unable to see clearly?"

"My judgment was impaired by an unwarranted and shameful vanity."

He heard the tremor in her voice. It touched him to the core. She *was* apologizing, and in a generous, self-deprecating, heartfelt way. "I don't know that your vanity was unwarranted," he said softly. "You were the loveliest, most breathtaking woman my nineteen-year-old eyes had ever seen."

Her eyes flew to his, wide with surprise. His quiet compliment, belated though it was, took her breath away. But a moment later, her awareness of the painful present reasserted itself. She smiled a wry, regretful smile. "Then *I'm* the one who's greatly changed, it seems."

He didn't answer. He didn't trust his voice. Her apology had caught him completely off guard. Her words had stirred a depth of feeling in him he didn't know he was capable of. He had to clench his fingers tightly on the reins so that she wouldn't see they were trembling.

He didn't understand her or himself. What had stirred her memory? And what was she trying to say in that oddly-worded apology? If she was truly sincere, how could he maintain the anger and resentment he'd built up against her? That resentment was the constant that had guided all his decisions since he first saw her on the coach. Even his betrothal had been instigated by his determination to keep

Miranda Pardew Velacott at a distance. A revised view
of her could seriously jeopardize his life! He had to *think*
before he could let himself warm toward her. And there
was no time now for thinking, for the horses were already
turning into the drive.

The stable man came running out as they drove up to the
front door. Barnaby threw him the reins. "Keep the horses
walking," he instructed as he lifted the sleeping child in his
arms. "I shall be taking them out again in half an hour."

"*Barnaby!* You're not going to look for the highwaymen,
are you?" Miranda asked in alarm.

She'd called him Barnaby. His heart leaped up to his throat
at the sound. But the emotion frightened him. *Good God*,
his mind said to him in disgust, *one brief expression of
regret from her lips, and you're putty in her hands!* He
had to take himself firmly in control, or he'd find himself
kissing her again with the same insane passion he'd felt
earlier. That kiss had been disturbing enough before, but
this time it would be unthinkable. He was now betrothed to
another. Such an incident could not be permitted to happen
again. Not now. Not ever.

He turned to look at her, making his whole face rigid with
disapproval. "Where I'm going, *Mrs. Velacott,* is none of
your affair," he said with chilling finality. He shifted the
boy to his shoulder and climbed down. Then he walked
round to her side and, with formal propriety, offered his
hand to help her down.

She could only gape at him, aghast. He'd done it *again*!
Without rhyme or reason, he'd switched his mood from
warmth to ice. One moment he was reminiscing about
how lovely she'd once been, and the next he was calling
her "Mrs. Velacott" in that disparaging way, a clear set-
down to retaliate for her calling him by his given name!
And telling her without roundaboutation to mind her own
business! If she lived a thousand years, she'd never learn
to understand him.

Angrily thrusting his hand aside, she climbed down from
the sleigh without his help. "I'll take the boy," she said,

making her voice as cold as his. "You're evidently in a hurry."

She took the boy in her arms, turned on her heel and stalked into the house without a backward look. *The man really is a churl!* she said to herself furiously. She'd tried to apologize. She'd tried her very best. If he chose to spurn her attempt at reconciliation, too bad for him. As far as she was concerned, he was not worth another thought. Or another tear.

· Twenty-three ·

THAT AFTERNOON WAS as good a time as any, Barnaby decided, to take care of the unfinished business of the highwaymen. His state of mind would benefit more from engaging in the perilous but straightforward adventure of tracking down the thieves than from remaining safely in an easy chair in the library brooding over this latest emotional upheaval. To solve the riddle of his confused feelings about Miranda would require maturity, mental clarity and serenity. To solve the problem of the highwaymen would require nothing more than a pistol.

Of course, he didn't have a pistol. But Terence surely had some weapons in this house. And Lawrence often brought a gun with him when he traveled. Barnaby, after a moment's thought, decided to ask Lawrence first. If he asked Terence, he'd lose precious time convincing the fellow not to come along. This was one adventure Barnaby was determined to engage in alone.

He found the Earl napping in his room. He shook the poor man heartlessly. "Wake up, Lawrence. Do you hear me? I need a pistol. Did you bring one?"

The Earl blinked. "Pistol?" he asked sleepily. "Yes, but . . . what for?"

"Where have you hidden it?" Barnaby persisted.

"In the second drawer of the dressing table. But why—?"

Barnaby strode across the room and found it. "Thank you, Lawrence. I shall restore it to you shortly."

"Wait just a moment!" the Earl ordered, now fully awake. "You can't have it till you tell me what it's for."

"I'll tell you all about it when I return, I promise."

Lawrence sat up and peered at his brother nervously. "It's those deuced highwaymen, isn't it? You're determined to wreak your revenge. Barnaby, I won't have it."

"It's not revenge," Barnaby assured him, his manner affably casual. "It's a purely materialistic act. I'm after the watch fob. I must have it back." He threw his brother a wide grin. "I'm sentimentally attached to it, since it was a gift from a beloved relative."

"Rubbish. I'll order another from my jeweler as soon as I return to Shallcross."

"I don't want another. It won't be the same." With a cheery wave, he started to the door.

Before reaching it, however, it flew open, and Honoria fluttered in, the wide skirt and sleeves of her dressing gown wafting on the air in her wake. "Lawrence, dearest, have you taken my wide-toothed comb? I can't seem to— Oh, *Barnaby*! *Here* you are!"

Barnaby surreptitiously hid the pistol behind him, out of Honoria's view. "Yes, here I am."

"Yes," Lawrence muttered irritably, "here he is, indeed. Perhaps you can talk sense to him."

"I always talk sense to him," Honoria retorted, completely missing her husband's point. "Barnaby, you are a rudesby. Why did you skip luncheon without a word to anyone? We all missed you. Livy didn't know what to do with herself. Where have you been hiding?"

"Nowhere in particular. I was out riding. But I can't stay here chatting. I must be off, so if you'll excuse me . . ."

"But Barnaby, you mustn't take off again," his sister-in-law cried in loud objection. "You *can't*."

"That's just what I've been telling him," the Earl growled.

Barnaby edged toward the door. "Why can't I?"

"You can't offer for a girl and then leave her constantly to her own devices," Honoria scolded. "It's rude and unkind."

Barnaby shrugged. "Can't be helped, my dear." He kissed her cheek and whisked himself out the door. But after taking a step down the corridor and hiding the pistol in an inner pocket of his coat, he turned back. "By the way, Honoria," he said from the doorway, "there's something I must ask you. Why on earth did you remind Mrs. Velacott about the Lydell ball?"

Honoria's eyebrows rose. "I *never* did! What makes you think—?"

"She suddenly indicated that she remembers what happened between us that evening. She actually apologized to me for it."

"*Did* she, indeed!" Honoria muttered tartly, not at all impressed. "Good of her, I must say."

"It *was* rather good of her, actually. She seemed truly to be ashamed of her younger self. I was quite . . . touched."

"Were you really?" Honoria peered at him through narrowed eyes. She had not forgotten Delia's comments about the governess. Could Delia be right? Was Miranda Pardew, of all women in the world, the proper partner for her beloved Barnaby? Was it possible that, underneath all the resentment, he actually harbored a *tendre* for the woman who'd spurned him?

"It seems strange, doesn't it," Barnaby was saying, "that, out of the blue, a woman would suddenly remember an eleven-year-old incident that could not have meant anything to her at the time?"

Honoria gave a troubled sigh. "If the answer to that question is important to you, my love, speak to Delia about it."

"Delia? Why Delia?"

"Well, you see, she . . . I . . . she has more . . . ah . . . insight into these matters than I." Honoria dropped her eyes from her brother-in-law's face and fingered the sleeves of her dressing gown uneasily, expecting him to demand to know why she'd discussed this matter with Delia at all. "You said you were in a hurry, didn't you, Barnaby? So why don't you save your questions for a more propitious time?"

Barnaby started to protest but changed his mind. He merely nodded and accepted the opportunity to take himself off.

After he'd gone, Honoria sank down on the side of her husband's bed, her eyes fixed on the door Barnaby had just closed behind him. "Do you think I made a mistake, Lawrence, pushing little Livy on him?"

"You didn't push," Lawrence protested. "You merely brought the girl here. Barnaby's the one who made the offer. But you do have a way of confusing me, my dear. I thought you were overjoyed over the boy's betrothal. Why are you suddenly apprehensive about it?"

Honoria eyed him for a moment, reluctant to admit her doubts about the girl she'd thrust under Barnaby's nose. "Something Delia said," she said at last. "She thinks Livy Ponsonby's a dead bore."

"Hmmm." The Earl scratched his nose and lowered his head but said nothing more.

"Lawrence!" Honoria knew him well enough to recognize the full meaning of the gesture. "*You* think so, *too*! Why didn't you *say* something to me?"

"Because, my dear, matchmaking is not in my line. You are the expert in affairs of the heart. When have I ever questioned your judgment in these matters?"

"Perhaps you *should* have questioned it. How shall you feel if I've made a dreadful mistake this time?"

"Naturally, I should be most distressed to see Barnaby unhappy. But, Honoria, it's time we both learned a lesson from all this. Barnaby has asked, time and again, that we permit him to manage his own life. I think, if we truly let him be, he will do very well for himself."

"Even if he's entangled in a mistaken betrothal?"

"Especially in that regard. For several years now, it's been obvious to me that Barnaby is better able to take care of himself than any of the rest of us. So leave the fellow free to make his own mistakes—and to correct them, too. That, mark my words, is the very best thing you can do for him."

· Twenty-four ·

THE SLEIGH SLID to a quiet stop in the small courtyard of the Deacon's Gate Inn, and Barnaby hopped down from the seat. The inn looked less inviting in the late-afternoon shadows than it had on the night, almost a fortnight ago, when its lights had glimmered out at him through the heavy snow. That night its appearance had signified much-needed warmth and comfort. Now it meant only a challenge.

Barnaby threw open the door, strode into the taproom with the sureness of familiarity, and took a seat at one of the three tables. Only one table was occupied, and that by a lone drinker, an elderly man bent over his tankard. He would not be in the way, Barnaby decided.

Barnaby did not have long to wait before Mrs. Hanlon approached. "Welcome, sir," she greeted in her cheery brogue, "an' what can I—?"

Barnaby got to his feet and smiled down at her.

The woman's face brightened in pleased surprise. "Why, it's Mr. Traherne, as I live an' breathe! What're ye doin' back 'ere again?"

Barnaby was glad it was Mrs. Hanlon rather than her husband. She would be easier to deal with. "I came to have a word with you, Mrs. Hanlon," he said quietly. "Will you kindly sit down with me?"

Mrs. Hanlon's face clouded, as if she suspected what was

to come, but she slid into a chair opposite him. "Are ye certain it's me ye want an' not me 'usband?"

"Yes, quite certain. Let's get right down to it, shall we? I remember, when we were last here, Mrs. Hanlon, hearing your husband say that the footpads always paid their shot in cash."

The woman mouth tightened. "Did 'e?"

"He did. One may assume from those words that the footpads have called at this taproom from time to time."

"I wouldn' assume that a-tall," she equivocated.

"I would. In fact, I'd wager a small fortune on it." He took out a handful of gold guineas and stacked them on the table before him. "I'd wager this small fortune that you know their hideaway."

Mrs. Hanlon eyed the gold pieces longingly. "Knowin' is one thing, an' tellin's another."

"Knowing without telling won't earn you a farthing, I'm afraid."

She shook her head. "You know what 'appens to anyone what blabs on 'em. Tellin's too dangerous, even fer a lovely pile o' gold like that."

"But your name will never pass my lips. My word on it. And they can't connect me with this place, for they have no idea I ever stayed here. They would guess I kept going north."

"That's true." She remained silent for a moment, considering the problem, her eyes fixed on the guineas. "There's a little tavern 'bout two miles west, on Deacon's Road, wi' three or four rooms upstairs. The rooms ain't available, 'cause they're permanently spoke fer, if ye take my meanin' "

"You mean they live there."

She shrugged. "It's a filthy 'ole, called the Blue Fox. Not near a main road, see, so the patrons 're on'y locals."

"A safe hideway, then."

She dropped her eyes. "So far."

He slid the pile of coins toward her, but kept his hand over them. "It's a *pair* we're speaking of, isn't it? One tall and broad, the other small in both height and breadth, named Japhet?"

She looked up at him in fright. "Y' ain't goin' t' ask me fer names, now! It wasn't part o' the bargain."

"No, no. But I must be certain I'm chasing the right pair. If my description matches what you know, simply nod."

She nodded.

He released the coins and rose. "Thank you, Mrs. Hanlon. I stand in your debt."

She was counting out the coins with greedy fingers. "No, I wouldn' say that, sir. This is 'andsome payment, I'd say. Very 'andsome indeed."

"Then, ma'am, perhaps you'll agree to do one more thing for me. If two brawny fellows come asking questions about my whereabouts—both as tall as I but a good bit broader— I'd be obliged if you'd deny ever having seen me."

She cocked her head at him suspiciously. "An' who might these brawny fellows be? Bow Street Runners?"

"No, not runners, but just as persistently annoying. They're my deuced brothers."

· Twenty-five ·

AT THE MANOR house it was not yet time to dress for dinner. Harry and his betrothed sat together in the small sitting room in a comfortable—and for a couple on the brink of matrimony, perfectly respectable—embrace, the man's arm lightly holding her round the waist and the lady's head resting on his broad shoulder. They were passing the time by discussing plans for their wedding, set for the opening of the London Season in spring. Lady Isabel's parents, who were very well to pass, were planning an elaborate affair for their only child, with four hundred invited guests. Harry, not at all shy, had no objection to the plans, but he loved to tease his bride-to-be by pretending to be appalled by the ostentation of large weddings and by constantly urging her to elope. "We could do it tonight," he was whispering into her ear. "I could wait under your window with the sleigh, you could slide down a rope-ladder made of Delia's best sheets—"

"Oh, *Harry*," his betrothed objected, laughing and pretending to push him away in punishment, "what a ridiculous notion! If you think I would consider dashing off to Gretna, catching my death in the cold and snow, and ruining my reputation in the bargain, you are much mistaken."

"Reputation!" Harry sneered. "How can your reputation compare to the sheer romance of running—?"

But before he could finish, the door burst open. "Harry," cried Terence from the doorway, "I think he's gone and done it!"

Harry dropped his hold on his betrothed and moved a discreet distance away. "Did no one teach you to knock, you blockhead?" was his greeting. "Isabel and I were planning an elopement."

"Sorry, Isabel," Terence said, "but this can't wait. I tell you, Harry, Barnaby's *done* it!"

"Done what? *Eloped?*"

"Harry, really!" Lady Isabel scolded. "You should know better. Livy Ponsonby would never—"

Terence smacked the heel of his hand against his forehead in impatience. "Will you *listen*? He's gone after the highwaymen!"

That made Harry snap to attention. He jumped up from the sofa in alarm. "Barnaby? All by himself?"

"Yes, just as he said he would."

"Damn the boy! How could he—?"

"Let's not stand here and discuss it, you slowtop. Let's go after him."

"Right!" Harry turned to his openmouthed betrothed. "You will excuse me, won't you, my love? I'll be back before morning, I promise."

"But Harry—!"

Before she could begin to enumerate her objections to this hasty action, the butler appeared in the doorway. "Madam sent me to tell you you're wanted in the drawing room, Mr. Traherne," he said to Terence. "At once."

Terence shook his head. "Not now, Cummings. Tell her I've gone off to help Barnaby. She'll understand."

"I'm afraid not, sir. This is urgent."

"Urgent? What can possibly be more urgent—?"

"Visitors," the butler said succinctly. "Lady Ponsonby and a young man. They both appear to be extremely upset, and Miss Ponsonby is having a fit of hysterics."

This did indeed sound urgent. Harry and Terence exchanged looks. "I suppose we ought—" Harry muttered.

"Of course we ought," Lady Isabel said with the decisiveness her rearing had bred in her and which had won her everything she'd ever wanted, including Harry Traherne. "Lead the way, Cummings," she ordered, sweeping to the door. "Lead the way."

In the drawing room, they were met with an ominous silence, except for the hiccuping sobs issuing from the chest of little Livy, who was huddled in an easy chair, her head buried in one of its wings. Sitting opposite her, erect and stern-faced, but dabbing at her eyes with a wet handkerchief, was a deep-bosomed matron who was apparently Lady Ponsonby, the weeping girl's mother. Standing at the window, his back stiff and his arms crossed over his chest, was a handsome, redheaded fellow who appeared to be in his mid-twenties. And leaning on the mantel, looking over the scene with a frown on her face but a strange, almost amused, glint in her eyes, was Delia Traherne.

Delia greeted her husband with a look that said, *Thank goodness you're here. Now you can take over.* Aloud, however, she merely made the introductions. "Lady Ponsonby, Mr. Ned Keswick, I'd like you to meet Lady Isabel Folley, my husband Terence Traherne and his brother Harry. Terence, dear," she added in a voice that was sugary-sweet, "we seem to be embroiled in a rather huge misunderstanding. Mr. Keswick and her ladyship are at odds on a point that is of concern to all of us. But perhaps I should say no more until Barnaby joins us."

"I could not find him, ma'am," the butler said from the doorway, where he'd lingered in hopes of catching some hint of the nature of the crisis. "Mr. Barnaby Traherne has apparently taken the sleigh and ridden out."

"I see." Delia expelled a sigh of disappointment. "Well, thank you, Cummings, you may go."

As soon as the door closed, Terence stepped forward. "May I be told about this 'point of concern' on which the gentleman and her ladyship are at odds?"

Delia nodded. "Mr. Keswick claims that Livy is *betrothed* to him."

"Betrothed?" Terence peered at his wife, trying to judge if this were some sort of joke.

But to Lady Ponsonby, it was no joke. She stiffened. "I unequivocally deny that claim," she said in a voice both quivery and firm. "Mr. Keswick is mistaken. How can there be a betrothal which is neither agreed to nor acknowledged by the girl's parents?"

"The *girl* acknowledged it," the young man shouted from his place at the window. "She accepted me, and she's of age."

"Now, just a moment, here," Harry interjected. "A girl can break a pledge of that sort, if she wishes. So that ends that."

"She never broke her pledge. Never!" The young man strode over to Livy's chair. "For heaven's sake, *tell* them, Livy! Pull yourself together! I'm here now. I'll protect you from your mother and anyone else who tries to bully you."

Livy's only response was an increase in the volume of her sobs.

"You're doing the bullying, you cad!" cried Lady Ponsonby.

"So, my dear," Delia said to Terence, "you see how matters stand."

Terence nodded. "Your Ladyship, Mr. Keswick, will you excuse the members of my family for a moment? I think we need some private conversation to determine how to proceed."

The four—Delia, Isabel, Terence and Harry—huddled together in the corridor. "What a fix!" Harry exclaimed. "Can't the girl be made to speak and explain herself?"

"She's been weeping ever since her mother arrived," Delia said, "and when her redheaded swain made his appearance, she became utterly incoherent."

"Are you saying they did not arrive together?" Isabel asked.

"They came in separate equipages."

"That means the roads are open to the south," Terence remarked.

"Of what relevance is that?" his wife demanded impatiently.

"None at all." Terence rubbed his chin, trying to make sense of this muddle. He couldn't help wondering how much his beloved brother would be hurt by this latest revelation. "Poor Barnaby." He sighed.

"Do you call him poor Barnaby because he has a rival," Delia asked dryly, "or because he's chosen such a watering-pot for a bride?"

Terence gave a short laugh. "Yes, on both counts."

"What has the Earl to say about this contretemps?" Isabel inquired.

"I haven't told him." Delia looked up at her husband worriedly. "Honoria may take this very much to heart. Perhaps we should wait until Barnaby gets here before we bring them into it."

Harry and Terence glanced at each other again. "Barnaby may not get back very soon," Harry said, attempting to break the news to his sister-in-law gently.

Delia looked from one brother to the other. "What do you mean? *How* soon is not very soon?"

"Perhaps," Terence muttered, "not until morning."

"*Morning*! Where on earth has he gone?"

Isabel cast a disparaging look at both the brothers. "What these hulking cawkers are too cowardly to tell you, Delia, is that Barnaby has gone after the highwaymen, and that *they* intend to go after Barnaby."

"Good God!" Delia threw her hands up in disgust. "Men!"

Terence put his hands on her shoulders. "It won't be so bad, my love. Give everyone dinner and send them off to bed. We'll fetch Barnaby back, and by morning we'll be able to settle the whole matter."

"Hmmm," Delia said, thinking over the possibilities. "I suppose that's all I *can* do. But if these new arrivals are to join us for dinner, I shall have to tell Lawrence and Honoria what's occurred."

"Tell them, then," said Terence, relieved to be free to make his escape and leave this mix-up behind. "Come, Harry, let's be off."

"Just fetch the fellow," Delia ordered, "and let the high-waymen *be*! If I discover that you've become embroiled in a shooting match with those miscreants, I warn you, Terence Traherne, that when I next lay eyes on you, I'll shoot you myself!"

· Twenty-six ·

THE BLUE FOX tavern was tucked away in a grove of trees, so far off the road that Barnaby drove right past it. It was dark by the time he found it, but not so dark that he couldn't see how squalid it was. Its sign hung crookedly from only one hinge, its courtyard was littered with debris that even the snow could not cover, its windows were so filthy that Barnaby could not see through them to the inside, and one of them was boarded up with such careless workmanship that not one of the roughly hewn slats lined up with its neighbor. It was through one of the gaps between those slats that Barnaby was able to get a glimpse of the scene within.

He'd hidden the sleigh in the trees and tethered the horses well out of sight of anyone entering or leaving the tavern. Now, his eye to the gap in the window-boarding, he was trying to discover what—and whom—he might be facing. Inside he could see a small, smoky taproom furnished with one long table and benches along its length. Half a dozen ill-clad patrons sprawled upon them. They were being served by a buxom barmaid in a dirty apron and beribboned cap, who evidently was not averse to being fondled by one and all. Barnaby studied the men at the table carefully, but he could not identify any of them. One smallish fellow, whose back was to the window, looked like Japhet, but the tall highwayman could have been any one of the others.

Calculating that, even if he were wrong about the identity of the small man, the risk of error was not great, he decided to proceed on the assumption that the fellow was Japhet. He lowered his hat over his forehead so that the brim shadowed his face, opened the door of the tavern and stepped inside. He found himself in a small vestibule lit by two candles burning in wall sconces. He blew them both out. Then he positioned himself just behind the doorway to the taproom and waited for the barmaid to walk by.

He did not have to wait long. As she sauntered by the doorway, carrying a lightly-loaded tray, he reached out, seized her arm and pulled her into the vestibule, catching the tray with his free hand. While she gasped in angry surprise, he set the tray on the floor. " 'Oo the devil are ye?" the girl demanded, trying to make him out in the shadowy hallway.

He stepped behind her, and holding her arms against her sides with one arm, he covered her mouth with his other hand. "Hush, me darlin', hush," he whispered in her ear in a soft Irish brogue. "There's a yellowboy for ye if ye keep your voice down an' do me a tiny favor. Hush, now, an' I'll let ye go." Slowly he released his hold on her mouth and waved a gold coin before her eyes.

She tried to get a glimpse of him but could not turn in his hold. "Who are ye? An' what do ye want o' me?"

"I want ye to go inside and tell Japhet there's a friend of his out here has a surprise for him."

"Whyn't ye tell 'im yersel'? 'E's right inside."

Barnaby smiled to himself. The risk had paid off. "I said it's a surprise," he whispered into the girl's ear. "Isn't it worth a gold piece to ye to play the game my way?"

"I s'pose so," she said dubiously, but as soon as he loosed his hold, she made a lunge for the coin.

He held it up out of her reach. "Now, me darlin', ye do know what ye're to say, don't ye?"

She took a close look at him, but his appearance meant

nothing to her. "I'm to say a friend o' his is waitin' outside wi' a surprise fer 'im."

"Yes. Exactly so." He gave her the coin, which she immediately tested with her teeth. Then he turned her about and pushed her toward the taproom door. "Hurry, now," he said, "like the sweet lamb ye are."

As soon as she crossed the threshold, he whisked himself outside to watch her through the gap in the window-boarding. He saw her come up to Japhet and tell him something. Then she pointed to the vestibule. He looked in that direction, shrugged and shook his head. She showed him the coin, tossed it up in the air triumphantly, caught it, pocketed it and sauntered off. *Come on*, Barnaby urged him silently. *No man of sense would give a barmaid a gold coin for nothing. Someone outside must have something of value for you. Come and see what a lovely surprise awaits you!*

As if his mind had received the message, Japhet got slowly to his feet and started toward the vestibule. Barnaby moved to the doorway and flattened himself against the outside wall just to the right of it. In a moment, the door opened and Japhet stepped outside. "Molly, you lying slut," he shouted, "there's nobody—"

"Yes, there is," said Barnaby, grabbing the little man's neck in the crook of his elbow and holding the pistol to his head. "Now, if you don't want a bullet in your noggin, you'll do what I say without a word."

"But who—?"

Barnaby tightened his hold and let his prisoner hear him cock the pistol. "I said without a word. Nod if you understand me."

Japhet nodded tensely.

"Good. Now, fellow, lie facedown on the ground, arms spread."

Japhet followed the order. Barnaby uncocked the pistol, stuck it in the waistband of his breeches, knelt down with his knee in the footpad's back, and took out two small lengths of rope, with which he first tied Japhet's hands tightly behind him and then bound his ankles. Then he dragged him to his feet. "Now, Japhet, tell me your partner's name."

"I . . . I ain't got no partner."

"The one who robbed the stagecoach with you about a fortnight ago. It must have been your last job, for there hasn't been much traffic since. His name, please."

"I don't know whut yer talkin' about. Ye mus' be mistakin' me."

Barnaby pulled out the pistol and held it to the miscreant's head again. "You evidently have a desire to die young. One more chance. His name, please."

"T-Timothy Cosh."

"You call him Tim, do you?"

"Sometimes. Mostly we call 'im Coshy."

"Good. Now, I'm going to help you to the tavern door, which you so carelessly left open, and you're going to call him. Loudly. Coshy, you'll say, there's something out here that you must see."

Japhet, shaking with fright, did what he was bid. Nervousness affected his voice, so the shout had to be done twice. When it was done, Barnaby pushed him down on the ground again and swiftly tied his mouth with a large handkerchief. Then he placed himself against the wall again, his pistol at the ready.

When Timothy Cosh stepped over the threshold, he didn't see a thing at first. When he saw Japhet trussed up and lying shivering on the ground, he gasped. In three quick steps, he came to his partner and knelt down. "Damn it, Japhet, what—?"

Then he heard the door close behind him and swung around. He found himself facing the barrel of a very deadly-looking pistol. "Oh, hell!" he cursed. "Who—?"

"Don't you remember me?" Barnaby asked. "You once relieved me of my very favorite gold watch."

Timothy Cosh groaned. "I remember. You was the bloke wi' the 'andy fists."

"That's right. Raise your hands, if you please. I want to see what you have in your pockets."

"I don't 'ave me pistol on me."

This proved to be true. "Now, Coshy, let me tell you what I have in mind. I'm going to allow you to go back inside and upstairs to the place you inhabit. There you will collect everything you stole from the stage that day and bring it all down in a sack. Meanwhile, I'll be holding this pistol against your partner's temple. If you don't come back by the time I count to one hundred, poor Japhet's brains will be spilled out all over the snow."

Japhet made little mewling sounds in his throat, and he wriggled his body around in hysterical fear.

"Japhet seems to understand me," Barnaby said to the other man. "Do you?"

"Yes, but I don't 'ave the loot no more. It's all in the 'ands o' me fence."

"No, it isn't. No fence could have come up from London through all that snow. Not yet."

"I ain't got nothin' left, I swear!" Coshy insisted. But his confederate on the ground groaned and wriggled with more hysteria than before.

"Of course, I can shoot you both right now—you first, Coshy—and go upstairs and see for myself."

"A'right, a'right, I'll go," the tall fellow muttered.

"I knew you would. But before you do, let me point out that if it should occur to you to bring a pistol down with you, or to enlist the assistance of any of your confederates inside, I shall have the pistol cocked. Even if someone shoots me in the back, my finger will be able to squeeze the trigger before I fall. So if you wish to see your friend alive when you return, you will refrain from any activity other than that which I've requested. Remember, you have only to the count of one hundred."

A most pathetic, pleading whimper issued from Japhet's throat. His partner looked down at him. "Stop whinin', ye numbskull. I ain't never let ye down afore, an' I won't do it now." With that, he turned and trudged back into the tavern and shut the door.

Barnaby wasted no time. He grasped the fallen Japhet

under the arms and dragged him across the small clearing and into the line of trees. There he took a place behind a tree and waited.

He didn't bother to count, but it seemed longer than two minutes before the door opened again. The tall highway-man stood silhouetted in the doorway, carrying a sack. He looked around the deserted clearing, bemused.

"Come out," Barnaby shouted. "I'm still here."

Timothy Cosh stepped over the threshold and out into the clearing. "Ye don't 'ave much trust in me, do ye?" he asked.

"Should I? Come into the center of the clearing and toss the sack over this way."

"Where's Japhet?"

"He's here, safe and well. Toss it!"

Coshy heaved it over, his reluctance apparent in every move he made.

"Good. Now, spread out your arms and lie facedown on the ground."

"What fer?"

"Do it!"

The footpad got down. Barnaby waited for several min-utes. There was no sound but a weak whimpering from Japhet. Finally, with his pistol poised, Barnaby stepped cautiously out from the protection of the trees and crossed the clearing to the prostrate Coshy. He was only a foot away from him when he thought he detected movement at the corner of the building on his right. Quickly he dropped down on his knees, one of them planted right on Coshy's back, and fired at the corner. A groaning cry (telling him he'd made his mark) coincided with a red flash of light, and a bullet whizzed by his ear. "Damn you, Cosh, you can't even be straight with your partner!" Barnaby swore, hastily trying to reload his pistol while keeping all his weight on the footpad's back.

"*Fire*, ye looby," Cosh shouted to someone at the tavern, "afore he reloads!"

There was another flash, this time from the other side, but the shot was wild. Cosh, no fool, knowing that Barnaby was still trying to reload, took the opportunity to try to wrench himself free. Heaving himself up, he dislodged Barnaby from his back and rolled over, reaching for a gun he'd hidden in his belt. But before he could pull it out, Barnaby, from his prone position, kicked his booted foot into the miscreant's chin and rolled over, swinging the butt of the pistol against Cosh's forehead. The man fell back unconscious.

Another shot rang out, this time from the left side of the tavern. Barnaby, shielding himself with the body of the unconscious highwayman, tried again to reload. But at that moment, he heard a burst of shots behind him, and two horsemen came galloping into the clearing and up to the tavern, shouting and shooting and making enough noise to wake the dead. They frightened every man who still lurked in or around the tavern. As Barnaby watched, three men ran from the place, one pulling a wounded man behind him, and disappeared into the trees. Meanwhile, the two horsemen pulled their horses to, wheeled about and rode toward him. By the time they reached him, Barnaby was on his feet and grinning. "You blasted gudgeons," he greeted his brothers, "can't you ever keep your noses out of my business?"

"We only came in at the finish," Harry chortled, leaping from the saddle and clapping Barnaby on the back.

"You seem to have done very well on your own," Terence grinned, sliding down and shaking his hand.

"Then why did you find it necessary to come after me?" Barnaby demanded.

"To bring you home. You're needed there, and at once," Terence informed him. "Emergency."

"Emergency!" Barnaby glared at him. "What rubbish!"

"It's not rubbish," Harry said. "There *is* an emergency."

"Truly?" Barnaby's face took on a look of alarm. "Not Jamie. Is he ill?"

"No, no. Nobody's ill. It's nothing like that," Terence assured him.

"Then what sort of emergency is it?"

"Delia will tell you all about it. So take yourself off, if you please."

"Dash it, Terence, you can see that I can't go right now. There are details to finish up. First, I must cart this fellow and his cohort, whom I have lying tied up in the woods, to the magistrate in Wymondham. Then, after I remove a certain watch and a cameo from that sack of loot over there, I intend to drop the rest into the nearest church poor box."

"Very commendable," Harry said.

"I suppose," Terence suggested tentatively, "that it would demean your triumph if we offered to assist in the finishing up."

"Assist?" Barnaby eyed him with suspicion.

"I could deal with the felons for you," Harry offered.

"And I can find the church poor box," Terence said. "In that way, Barnaby—with your permission, of course—we could free you to go through the sack for your treasures and take yourself home."

Barnaby shrugged his agreement, and the three cheerfully set about the "finishing up." After they'd trussed up the pair of highwaymen and sorted through the loot, they agreed that Harry would transport the footpads in the sleigh, with Terence and Barnaby making their separate ways home on horseback. Barnaby was the first to mount. He looked down from the horse at the two devoted brothers smiling proudly up at him. "Dash it all," he said with a happy sigh, "it's been a ripping adventure. The first one of this sort you permitted me to execute on my own."

"You don't have to thank us," Harry taunted. "We were glad to do it."

Barnaby shook his head. "Impossible. You're both impossible." He spurred his horse and started off. "But next time," he threw back over his shoulder, "if you don't want a pair of bloody noses, you'd better wait for me at home."

· Twenty-seven ·

MIRANDA HAD HAD a difficult time getting her charges to go to sleep. Rumors that their uncle had ridden off to capture the highwaymen were circulating throughout the house, and the boys had begged to be allowed to stay awake for his return. She'd had to tell them six fairy tales and invent a new, utterly fantastical adventure of Robin Hood before she was able to settle them down for the night.

She, too, would not be able to shut her eyes this night, she realized. The day had been too disturbing, what with Jamie's running away, and her set-to with his uncle. And now this rumor of his going off to find the highwaymen. She wondered how much she was to blame. If she only hadn't mentioned the blasted cameo!

Then, to add to her distress, she'd heard the rumor concerning the new arrivals, Lady Ponsonby and a redheaded young man. What if the rumors were true that the fellow was Livy's betrothed? What sort of scrape had Livy fallen into? And would Barnaby be badly hurt by it?

There was no point in trying to sleep. She would only lie in bed and toss about, worrying about Barnaby Traherne, although he, on his part, would not be wasting a thought on her. Nevertheless, going to bed would only lead to a wallow in painful and useless self-pity. So, instead of retiring, she decided to go down to the kitchen and make herself a pot of tea. There was nothing like tea to settle one's nerves.

She expected the kitchen to be deserted by this time, for the entire household had retired early, but she found Lady Shallcross's abigail there before her. The girl, in her nightclothes, and with her hair tied all over with rags, was setting a tea tray for her mistress, her pretty, bow-shaped mouth distorted by a sullen frown. "Everythin's at sixes and sevens today," the girl complained. "Her ladyship's sore distressed—not as I blame her with all that's happenin'—but she waked me from a sound sleep, askin' for some tea. So what am I to do, I ask you, with my hair in rags an' my eyes half shut? Can I bring her tea lookin' like this?"

"I'm still dressed," Miranda said. "Let me take it to her."

The girl's surly expression cleared at once. "Oh, *would* ye, Mrs. Velacott? I'd be ever so grateful."

Miranda, the tea tray in hand, tapped at Honoria's bedroom door. "Come in, come in," came a querulous voice from within.

She found Honoria lying on her bed with eyes shut, pressing a wet cloth to her forehead. "Lady Shallcross!" she exclaimed. "Are you ill?"

Honoria's eyes flew open. "Mrs. Velacott? Is that you?"

"Yes, ma'am. I've brought you your tea."

"But my Betty should not have asked you to take her task," Honoria said, throwing off the cloth and sitting up. "It's a dreadful imposition."

"Not at all. I was happy to do it. Will you take your tea in bed, Your Ladyship, or shall I set it up for you here on this little table near the fire?"

Honoria tossed off her covers and climbed down from the bed. "On the table, please, if you will consent to join me. There are some teacups on the mantel."

Miranda shook her head. "It's not necessary to give me tea, Lady Shallcross. I—"

"Please," Honoria begged, hastily pulling another chair over to the table. "I have been wishing to speak to you all day."

Both women, eyeing each other uneasily, took seats across from each other at the little table. No words were exchanged while Miranda poured the tea, but then, with her teacup in hand, Honoria looked across at her visitor and frowned. "I never liked you, you know. Never. Even *before* the Lydell ball."

Miranda blinked at her, feeling as if she'd been slapped, but she recovered her composure in a moment. "No, of course you didn't," she said bluntly. "I don't blame you, ma'am, not a bit. I was a dreadful, vain, self-centered, foolish creature."

"Yes, you were," Honoria agreed. "My word for you was flibbertigibbet."

Miranda smiled. "I can think of many worse words for me." She stirred her tea thoughtfully, her smile fading. "I don't remember much about the Lydell ball," she admitted, "but I remember enough to realize that what I did was quite unforgivable. In your place, I would not like me, either."

Honoria was touched by the apology. "Very few things in this life are unforgivable," she said generously, her eyes searching the younger woman's face. Miranda Pardew was still lovely, she admitted to herself. And her frankness was refreshing. And she was certainly easier to talk to than the tongue-tied Livy Ponsonby. Honoria sighed deeply. "In regard to the Lydell ball," she confessed, "Delia says I've made much too much of an insignificant incident."

"Oh, no, I don't agree. If your brother-in-law was greatly affected by it, how can it be insignificant?"

"Yes, that's *just* how I feel! How generous of you to grant that!" She set her cup down on the table and stirred her tea reflectively. "But in a sense, Delia may be right. Perhaps the effect on Barnaby was, in the end, a beneficial one. Everyone seems to be convinced that he's not at all shy any more. And he's turned out to be a fine and successful man, a really *good* man, wouldn't you say so?"

Miranda dropped her eyes. "He certainly seems so to me."

"Does he? Truly?" Honoria peered closely at the young woman opposite her. She hoped that Miranda would say more. If there was anything she liked to hear, it was praise for her beloved Barnaby.

"Oh, yes," Miranda said, her lips curling into a reflective smile as the many qualities that had endeared Barnaby to her flew into her mind. "He's so clever and quick-witted and . . ." She stared into the fire with unseeing eyes, her heart swelling with fondness and a strange sort of pride. " . . . and very brave, of course. Fearless, almost . . ."

Honoria beamed. "And handsome, wouldn't you say?"

"Handsome, of course. And so devoted to his family, and . . ."

"And . . ." Honoria prodded.

"And spontaneous . . . impulsive, I mean . . ."

That surprised Honoria. "Impulsive? My Barnaby?"

"Yes. At least, he seems so to me."

"Does he? In what way?"

"Well, for instance, he once . . ." Blushing, she quickly picked up her cup and took a sip, berating herself for going too far. "No, never mind," she murmured in embarrassment.

"No, please, Miranda," Honoria urged, "don't be shy with me. He once what?"

Miranda glanced up at her and quickly looked down again. "He once . . . very impulsively— Oh, dear, I don't know why I'm telling you this!"

"Please go on, my dear. You can't imagine how much this talk means to me."

"He . . . kissed me."

"You don't say! When did he do that?"

"Just a few days ago. But you mustn't think . . . it was not . . . you mustn't make too much of it. As soon as he'd done it, he thought better of it. I only mention it to show his . . . his . . ."

"His spontaneity. I quite understand." Honoria smiled, wondering what Delia might make of that information. But it wouldn't do to press Miranda on the matter now. She was still red-cheeked over having mentioned the incident. "So you think him impulsive. And what else?"

"What else?" Miranda echoed, still too embarrassed to think clearly.

"Some young women call him forbidding. Would you describe him so?"

"Forbidding?" Miranda recovered herself with a start. Why had she been so loose of tongue with this woman who claimed to dislike her? And why had she revealed so much? But Honoria's warm and motherly manner made it difficult not to open up to her. "Yes, I'd say he's forbidding sometimes. He has a frown that can chill one's blood."

Honoria, remembering a similar conversation with Livy, was enchanted with Miranda's very different, very honest responses. "Then you wouldn't call him kind?"

"No, I wouldn't say he was kind," Miranda said with a rueful smile. "At least, he's not very kind to me."

"Oh? Isn't he?"

"No, not at all. But then, who can blame him? At first, at the inn, I believed him to be the worst of rudesbys. But now that I know the circumstances, I understand why he's often unkind."

"Oh, but that is really too bad." Honoria threw Miranda a darting glance. "Delia will be disappointed."

"*Delia*? Really? Why?"

"She believes that you and Barnaby would be well suited."

Miranda's eyes widened. "She *does*? How very astounding!"

"Isn't it? In truth, when she said it, I was convinced she was quite mad. But lately, I've not been so certain."

Miranda's breath caught in her throat, and she felt her fingers begin to tremble. "Lady Shallcross! You're not suggesting, are you, that you, *too*—?" She put a shaking hand to her forehead. "But you said you never liked me."

"Not until now." Honoria gazed with new eyes at the woman she'd so long disliked. All Miranda's comments had been honest and modest and very satisfying. Honoria had not enjoyed a conversation so much in years. *Good God*, she thought, *Delia is right about the girl after all*. Miranda Pardew might have been a flibbertigibbet, but Miranda Velacott was someone else entirely. This one— she had to admit—was a delight.

"But you . . . you *can't* like me!" Miranda was saying.

"Why not? If you can change, so can I. Besides, I don't have to like you. Barnaby has to."

"What are you saying?" Miranda, already shaken not only by Honoria's unexpected kindness but by these astounding revelations, felt her eyes fill up with the tears she'd suppressed all day long. Barnaby's icy words—the rude barbs he'd thrown at her this very afternoon—now rang in her ears in painful counterpoint to his sister-in-law's warmth. "But I've already told you," she said, her voice choked, "Barnaby hates me."

Honoria nodded sadly. "Yes, I suppose he does. And I suppose you dislike him, too."

"I?" She stared across the table into Honoria's soft, kind eyes. "Dislike him? No, I w-wouldn't say *that*, ma'am." The tears began to spill down her cheeks, and overwhelmed with emotion, she dropped her head in her arms right there on the table. "I l-love him!"

Honoria clutched her hands to her breast, astonished and touched to the heart. The anger and resentment that had built up for years seemed to fall away. Tenderly, with a heart aching with regret, she reached over and gently smoothed Miranda's lovely hair. "Oh, my poor dear!" she murmured.

Miranda looked up. "You are very k-kind," she whispered. "I'm so ashamed. I shouldn't have revealed—"

"Of course you should. I'm glad you told me." She pulled a handkerchief from her sleeve and wiped the younger woman's cheeks. "I only wish I could offer more than this handkerchief to dry your tears."

"You have. You can't know how much! I've had no one to open my heart to for a long, long time."

"Oh, my dear!" Honoria held the handkerchief to her own eyes. "It has just occurred to me that you could have been the daughter I always dreamed of!"

It was true, Honoria realized with a shock. Miranda Pardew Velacott, of all the women in the world, was just the sort of woman that Barnaby—and she herself—could love. Her throat choked with the painful knowledge that she'd closed her mind for too long . . . and that all her actions in regard to Barnaby's prospects for wedlock had been nothing but dreadful blunders.

· Twenty-eight ·

BARNABY RODE THROUGH through the night toward his brother's manor house, feeling as elated as any soldier after a battle won. Though the cold wind nipped at his nose and froze his fingers, and though the horse had to pick his way carefully through the snow and could not be made to gallop, Barnaby's spirits soared. He even sang for a while, an old Scottish air that Honoria used to sing to him when he was a child. Every once in a while, he'd put his hand in his pocket and finger the trophies that he'd won for himself this night: the watch and fob, and Miranda's cameo. The felons had broken the chain on which the cameo had hung, but he could fix it. Every time his fingers touched the little trinket, he smiled to himself. He couldn't wait to see her face when he dropped it into her lap.

But as he drew closer to the house, his spirits waned, and a depression, as chilling as the night air, enveloped him. At first he didn't recognize the cause, but after thinking about it for a while, he knew what it was. He was riding home to Livy Ponsonby, not Miranda.

Here in the icy darkness the truth became blindingly clear. The prospect of bringing Miranda back her cameo brought him a singing joy; the prospect of bringing himself to Livy brought a smothering gloom.

Not that these feelings made any sense. The fact was that Livy had accepted him; Miranda never would. Besides, he was convinced that Livy was everything a bride should be: pretty and gentle and agreeable and sweet. On the other hand, she was also tongue-tied and conventional and unsurprising and dull. Miranda was just the opposite: shocking, argumentative, insulting, dangerous and . . . and more exciting than any woman he'd ever met. That was the crux of it, he realized. Livy was—he had to admit it—tiresome. And Miranda was . . . dazzling.

That was the word. Every encounter he'd had with her dazzled him. Riding with her in the carriage, tied with her to the tree, playing cards with her at the inn, arguing with her about Jamie—every one of those moments had set his blood dancing in his veins. And kissing her had been . . . well, even "dazzling" was an inadequate word for *that*.

He'd loved her since he was a boy of nineteen, he knew that now. Some part of his mind had held on to his boyhood infatuation with an unshakable tenacity, becoming with time an unacknowledged conviction that she was the only woman he would ever truly love. And though she had not responded to him when he was young, she was different now. She had even, he believed, occasionally shown a liking for him. There had been warmth in her eyes from time to time, but each time he'd seen it, he'd stupidly cut her down. Even when he'd kissed her and—had he imagined it?—she'd melted in his arms, he'd pushed her away. Why on earth had he done it?

He tried to reconstruct his thinking from the time he'd rediscovered her in the carriage. The incident at the Lydell ball was the problem, of course. He'd kept it in his mind every time he saw her, a stubborn memory that had stood between them, as thick and impenetrable as a wall. He'd used it as a shield to protect himself from pain. How stupid! Didn't he know he was no longer a vulnerable boy? He'd long since learned how to handle hurt. What was he afraid of? True, Miranda was a challenge to his manhood, but he didn't meet the other challenges of his life so fearfully. No one could say that Barnaby Traherne lacked courage. Why had he turned cowardly with Miranda?

Instead of making a mature attempt to win her, he'd thought only of taking revenge, of giving her a set-down to equal the one she'd given him. In seeking an idiotic revenge for a minor insult, he'd made a major blunder. He'd lost his chance.

He put his hand in his pocket and fingered the little cameo once more. He pictured the chain hanging round her marvelous throat and the cameo lying between the curves of her breasts. The image made him dizzy with desire. That settled it. He could not—would not!—give up the girl he'd wanted for so long, not without a fight. After all, he was not yet wed. The holiday was not yet over. There was still time.

· Twenty-nine ·

MIRANDA AWOKE THE next morning with a feeling of bubbling anticipation. She could not account for it, but it was quite real. She drew back the curtains and discovered a day that matched her mood. The snow sparkled in the brightest sunlight she'd seen since her arrival, and the sky reflected back that sparkle with a crystalline-blue gleam. In the distance, she could see a wagon moving along the road, indicating that traffic was returning to normal. And somewhere nearby, a hardy winter bird was chirping excitedly, the chirp an embodiment in sound of what she herself was feeling inside.

But neither the bird nor the sky nor the glinting snow could account for her sense of tingling excitement. Of course, her conversation with Lady Shallcross last night could have something to do with it. Lady Shallcross had indicated that both she and Delia believed Miranda to be a more suitable wife to Barnaby than Livy Ponsonby. That *anyone* could wish to pair her with Barnaby Traherne was the outside of enough, but that the two women closest to Barnaby wished it quite took her breath away.

But of course, if one thought more carefully about it, the idea was ridiculous. Barnaby would never learn to like her. Besides, he was betrothed. It would be best to put such thoughts out of her mind.

She dressed quickly, for she had a great deal to do to get ready for the day's studies, but when she hurriedly threw open her door, she heard a strange rattle. Something was hanging on her outer doorknob. She looked down curiously and discovered—hanging by its chain, with a little note pinned to it—her cameo!

Her heart leaped into her throat. He'd recovered it! Barnaby himself! Staring down at the bauble, she felt like Elaine of Astolat, or even Queen Guinevere herself. Barnaby had been her knight on a quest. He'd tracked the dragon to its lair and recovered his lady's talisman! Now that it was over, and the knight was apparently unhurt, the idea of the quest delighted her. *And oh*, she thought, *how thrilled the boys will be to hear about it!*

With eager fingers, she unpinned the note and opened it, and her eyes flew over the words. *It is customary*, he'd written, *for the recoverer of a treasure to receive a reward. I shall be coming, in due course, to claim one. I hope you can think of something suitable, but if you can't, I have one or two suggestions.*

She clutched the trinket to her bosom, her spirit soaring. Even the note had the quality of knightly romance: the triumphant knight coming to claim his prize. Could it be that her feelings on awakening had been prophetic—that this was going to be a very exciting day?

But no, she warned herself. Barnaby was no knight and she was no prize. His recovery of her cameo was a gesture. It was a kind and generous gesture, of course, but nothing more. She should not make too much of it. Later, when the boys took their recess, she would go downstairs, thank him nicely and make an end of it.

But he was asking for a reward. What did he mean? He knew she had nothing to give him. Was he joking? But even if he were, she wanted to give him something tangible as a symbol of her gratitude. Would her finest, lace-edged handkerchief be acceptable? It was a modest reward, but it would have to do.

With these sobering thoughts, she was able to bring her spirits back down to earth. She had work to do.

On the floor below, at that very moment, all Barnaby's brothers, both his sisters-in-law, and Lady Isabel, were gathered in his bedroom. They surrounded the bed where he was soundly asleep. "Wake up, you gudgeon," Harry shouted into the sleeper's ear.

Barnaby sat up with a start. "What—?"

"Congratulations!" they all shouted, bending over him and embracing him all at once. Then they admitted Cummings into the room. The butler carried a tray holding glasses and a bottle of champagne. The Earl accepted the honor of opening the bottle, and the bubbling liquid was poured. Toasts were drunk until they ran out of words and drink.

Then Terence insisted that the hero make a speech. Barnaby, dizzy from the abrupt awakening and the early-morning imbibing, got up on his bed on two wobbly legs. "Ladies and gentlemen," he said, grinning sheepishly, "although I thank you for your good wishes, I hope you all will acknowledge that if you'd left me to my own devices before this, I'd have been a hero long ago." And with that, amid much laughter and applause, he fell forward on his face.

Delia, whose feet were always on the ground, took this opportunity to bring the roisterers back to earth. "Enough of this gaiety," she said sternly, urging them out of the room. "It's time to return to reality. You all must go down to the breakfast room, to entertain our visitors. Livy and her guests must be wondering what's become of us. Meanwhile, I shall inform Sir Hero about what awaits him down below."

By the time a sobered Barnaby had dressed and presented himself in the breakfast room, all signs of gaiety were gone. The large, round family breakfast table was surrounded by gloomy faces. Livy, still red-eyed, was no longer weeping, but she looked as if she might burst into tears again at a moment's notice. Her mother stood over her, with a hand on her shoulder, as if she didn't trust the girl out of her clutches. Ned Keswick, looking white about the mouth, as if his teeth had been clenched all night, stood leaning on the mantel, his eyes fixed on the girl he'd come to claim.

Barnaby regarded all of them. "Good morning," he said cheerfully. "I don't think there's a need for such long faces. This problem, if I understand it rightly, will not be difficult to solve."

"Oh, it won't, won't it?" Mr. Keswick snapped. "And how would you solve it if you were me, and you'd found out your betrothed had given her promise to another?"

Lady Ponsonby sidled across the room and took Barnaby's arm. "Please excuse this embarrassing scene, dear boy," she cooed, a smile on her face that was as false as it was inappropriate. "Mr. Keswick has no claim, I assure you. My dearest girl was swayed by a stroll in the moonlight, and she made promises to that fellow that she did not mean. She hadn't yet met you! She feels quite differently now and has a sincere desire to be your bride."

"That, ma'am, is a deuced lie!" Mr. Keswick exclaimed. "You are forcing the girl into a betrothal she does not want."

"But why would Lady Ponsonby *do* that?" the Earl asked in honest confusion. "Why force a girl to wed against her wishes?"

"Because she thinks your brother is a better catch than I!" Keswick said bitterly. "He's a Traherne of Shallcross, and I am in trade. It doesn't matter that my father's cotton mill will someday make it possible for me to provide more luxuries for her than a duke could. I'm in trade, and that makes me scum!"

"You're n-not scum!" little Livy muttered. They were the first words she'd spoken since her mother's arrival.

"Now, now, my sweet," her mother twittered nervously, "you must let me do the talking if you want to get out of this fix."

"I don't see that there's any fix at all," Barnaby said, removing his arm from Lady Ponsonby's grip. He strode over to the chair where Livy sat and knelt down beside her. "Livy, my dear, that afternoon in the library when I made you an offer, you looked as if you wanted to burst into tears. Do you remember that?"

Livy kept her head lowered and her eyes veiled, but she nodded.

"Was it Mr. Keswick you were thinking of then?"

She nodded again.

"Are you in love with Mr. Keswick?"

"Livy—!" her mother said warningly.

Barnaby threw Lady Ponsonby one of his daunting frowns. "I think it would be better, ma'am, if you said nothing more. Now, Livy, before you answer me, let me tell you—and your mother—that I am far from rich, that I am the fourth son of an earl with three very healthy brothers, so that the likelihood of my ever winning a title is so remote as to be unthinkable, and that professionally I am a mere public servant. Mr. Keswick, on the other hand, is young, handsome and, I gather, will one day be rich enough to buy himself a title. Am I right, Mr. Keswick?"

Redheaded Ned blinked at him in some surprise. "I think you put that very well."

"Now, then, Livy, let me ask you again. Are you in love with Mr. Keswick?"

A tense silence filled the room as every eye was fixed on Livy's bent head. She turned slowly in her chair. "I think I . . . love you *both*!" she stammered. "P-positively."

There was a universal groan. Barnaby winced. But for Mr. Keswick, this was the last straw. "Balderdash!" he exploded, and striding across the room, he pushed Barnaby aside, pulled Livy to her feet and took her in his arms. "You goose," he said firmly, "you do *not* love us both!" And he planted a very businesslike kiss on her mouth.

Livy did not struggle, nor did anyone in the room make a move to stop this flagrantly vulgar act. It was many moments before Ned Keswick let her go. When he did, Livy turned to Barnaby, her eyes shining. "I do love you both," she said, "but I . . . think I . . . love my Neddy more."

"Aha! That's my girl!" Ned crowed. He lifted her up in his arms and swung her round in triumph. "Now you and

I are going straight to Gretna." Without another word, and with only the merest nod to his swooning mother-in-law-to-be, he carried Livy from the room—and from the house.

Delia called out for Cummings to come running, and she went quickly to Lady Ponsonby's side. "Now, now, Your Ladyship, please don't take on," she soothed gently, helping the defeated woman to a chair and holding a glass of water to her pale lips. "Here, take a sip, do! As soon as you feel able to stand, we'll help you upstairs. A bit of a rest, and you'll find yourself perfectly well restored."

"Restored?" the woman cried. "How can you say so? My daughter is eloping with a *tradesman*!"

"That tradesman," Delia said, taking her under one arm while Cummings took the other, and walking her to the door, "seems a very admirable specimen to me. A more dashing, romantic fellow has never crossed this threshold. In fact," she added, throwing Terence a glinting glance over her shoulder, "if I were a free woman, I might have tried to win him for myself."

All the other members of Barnaby's family, fearful that the incident had made him unhappy, tried to hide their concern by busily attacking their breakfasts. Barnaby, watching them, wanted to laugh aloud, but he put on as somber an expression as possible, went over to Honoria and took her hand. "I hope, dearest, that you're not too deeply overset by this turnabout," he said, patting her shoulder affectionately.

"I? Certainly not," she assured him, searching his face in a vain attempt to read his emotions. "It is *you*—! How unfair that you should have to bear another . . . another . . ."

"Another set-down? Yes, can you believe such deuced bad luck?" But the twinkle in his eye belied his words. He leaned down and kissed his sister-in-law's cheek. "But I expect I'll learn to bear my loss." He sauntered to the door with a decidedly cheerful step. "I'm sure I'll learn to bear it passably well. In time."

· Thirty ·

HE WENT WHISTLING down the hall, his step as light as his heart. He felt as if a terrible weight had been lifted from his chest. He was free to pursue his dream, and to that end, he intended to go upstairs and face Miranda Pardew. But as he rounded the newel post and put a foot on the first step, he came face-to-face with her. "Oh! Mi— Mrs. Velacott!" he stammered. *Confound it,* he swore to himself, *whenever I come upon her unexpectedly, I'm a bubble-brained nineteen-year-old again!*

"Mr. Traherne," she greeted him, sounding a little breathless, "I was just coming to look for you."

"And I you." He laughed.

"About the reward," they said together.

She stood a step above him, so that they were face-to-face, eye-to-eye. "I do thank you," she said, dropping her eyes from the intensity of his stare. "I don't know what happened, but I do know that tracking down the robbers and confronting them couldn't have been easy."

"It was an adventure I very much enjoyed. But much too much ado has been made of it, so let's not dwell on the details."

"Very well, if you don't wish to speak of it now. But the boys are agog. You must come up and tell them about it."

"I will. Later. Right now, I'm more interested in what you've decided should be my reward."

She put her hand in her pocket and drew out a small, neatly folded, lacy handkerchief. "I haven't anything of real value, as you know," she said, holding it out to him, "but I hope that this will serve."

He looked up from her offering to where the cameo lay between the swells of her breasts and up to her shapely throat, her slightly-pointed chin, the full lips that were beginning to tremble under his scrutiny, and to her lovely, speaking eyes that at this moment would not tell him anything. And he shook his head. "A handkerchief," he said in a low voice, "is not quite what I had in mind."

"Then, what—?"

"I think you can guess," he said, and grinning boyishly, he pulled her to him and kissed her, eagerly, hungrily, but cleanly, without guilt or fear of being hurt by it. He felt her stiffen in resistance, but after a moment she swayed in his arms and seemed to melt, and he heard a little moan deep in her throat. *Oh, God, she does love me,* his heart sang.

But at that moment, she pushed him away with such force that he tottered back down the step. It reminded him of tripping down the rise of that platform at the Lydell ball. She was *playing* with him again! He was eleven years older and making the same fool of himself. And the pain of it was every bit as strong as ever!

He looked up at her, stung. But she didn't look in the least triumphant. She was backing up the stairs, rubbing away his kiss from her mouth with the back of her hand, her eyes wide with a pain as great as his. "That was cruel!" she said hoarsely. "Cruel and beastly! Lady Shallcross says you are kind, but I don't believe you capable of kindness." And she turned and ran up the stairs.

He didn't understand her. "Miranda, wait!" he croaked, stumbling after her. "I didn't mean to—" He caught up with her at the landing and grasped her arms. "Confound it, Miranda, how can you think me beastly?" he asked, gasping for breath. "I only thought . . . for a reward . . ."

"All right, then, you've had your reward! Let me go!"

"But you don't understand. I haven't yet—"

"Oh, haven't you? Well, it's all the reward you're going to get! Let your little Livy reward you!" She pulled off the cameo, breaking the chain, and threw it at him. "Here! If you must be rewarded for it that way, I don't want it!"

He gaped after her as she ran round to the second flight and disappeared from his view, and a sense of what had hurt her broke upon him. *Lord*, he thought, *I am a fool.* He'd done it backwards. He should have explained his feelings to her first and *then* kissed her. How could he have expected her to understand all the cowardly vacillations that had tormented him since he'd seen her on the stagecoach?

But I shall not be a coward again, he swore, and he dashed up the second flight, taking the steps three at a time. He almost caught up with her on the third flight, but she was too fleet for him and had almost reached the next landing. He reached up, caught her ankle and pulled her down. She twisted herself around and beat at his chest with her fists, tears coursing down her cheeks. "Let me up!" she muttered through clenched teeth. "Haven't you humiliated me enough?"

Holding her fast with his body, he caught her fists in his hands. "Damnation, Miranda, will you listen to me? You don't understand—"

"Yes, I do. It's revenge. You're obsessed with revenge. You had to take revenge on the footpads, and you have to have your revenge on me, for what I did to you eleven years ago."

"Miranda, please," he pleaded, trying to keep her from wriggling out of his hold. "It's not—! Won't you—?"

"Don't you see that you've already succeeded? I've been quite adequately set down. I'm crying. I'm humiliated. I'm hurt. So we're even. Let me up!"

"I'm not trying to get even. I love you! I'm trying to *win* you, don't you understand?"

She stopped wriggling. "I don't know what you're talking about. You're betrothed, aren't you?"

"No, I'm not. Livy has run off with another. A redheaded Midas called Keswick."

"Oh?" She blinked at him, arrested, her lips parted in a kind of suspended animation.

"And let me tell you, ma'am, that when he kissed Livy, *she* didn't push him away. She leaped into his arms and let him carry her off to Gretna."

"Did she?" She wriggled one hand free and wiped her cheeks with the back of it. "I'm . . . sorry."

"Don't be sorry. I only offered for her because I was afraid of you."

"Afraid of me? Why?"

"Because I felt such a fool for loving you all these years. Because you're still so beautiful. Because I was sure you'd rebuff me again."

She gulped back what was left of her tears. "You certainly don't appear to be afraid today. Kissing me on the stairs like a lecher with a kitchen maid! And holding me down on these uncomfortable stairs in this humiliating way. Let me up!"

"Very well, I will if you wish it. But then, will you agree to give me another chance? Please, Miranda, let me begin again. From the very beginning. So that we may meet properly this time."

She did not answer, but he got up and helped her to her feet. "Miss Miranda Pardew?" he asked, making a slight bow. "I was wondering if I might have this dance."

Her lips turned up in the slightest of smiles. "But my dance card is filled, sir. Don't you know that it's only maiden aunts and wallflowers who don't have their cards filled by this time? Do I look like a wallflower to you?"

"Oh, I know your card is filled, ma'am. But I hoped that, when you understood that my heart is bursting with the desire for you to dance with me, you would ignore your other partners and, in pity if for no other reason, choose me."

"That is a most touching invitation, sir, but I don't know even know your name."

"Does it matter? We can dance together *incognito*."

She slipped her hand in his. "Then lead the way, sir. I am yours, at least for the duration of one dance."

He led her down the stairs and through the hallway to the library, not saying a word. When he'd closed the door, he turned to face her. "Listen, Miss Pardew. Do you hear the music? It's a waltz." He slipped his arm about her waist. "Do you waltz, ma'am?"

"A waltz is rather daring for an inexperienced young man like yourself, isn't it?"

"When you know me better, you'll discover that underneath this rather cowardly, sheepish exterior, I *can* be rather daring," he said, sweeping her round the room in time to the music in his head.

When they'd grown so dizzy that the room spun around, they stopped dancing, but they clung to each other to steady themselves. "Is the dance over?" she asked in a whisper.

"I want it to go on forever, but it's not for me to say." He peered down into her face intently. "*Is* it over?"

She shook her head, threw her arms about his neck and drew his head down to hers. The kiss was long, and deep, and told him everything he needed to know—they'd come through the miasma of misunderstandings and confused emotions that had surrounded them for far too long, and had found each other at last.

The kiss might have gone on endlessly, but the library door flew open. "I say, Barnaby," said the Earl from the threshold, "Honoria has been looking for— Oh!"

Barnaby lifted his head. "Looking for me?"

"Well, er . . . I don't suppose it was very urgent," the Earl muttered in embarrassment.

Just then, Harry appeared in the doorway. "How about a game of billiards, old fellow? Isabel is busy with her hair, and I— Oh, am I interrupting something?"

As if on cue, Terence put his head in the door. "Barnaby, are you in here? Delia said to tell you that Lady Ponsonby is taking her leave and— Oh, I say! What's going on here?"

Barnaby, refusing to release the blushing Miranda from his hold, looked over at his three brothers crowded in the doorway and fixed them with one of his famous glowers. "I might have known the three of you would find a way to interfere. What is going on here is a private matter. I'm trying to make an *offer* to this young lady."

"An offer?" the Earl asked, his face lighting up.

"I say!" exclaimed Terence, awestruck.

"Oh, capital!" Harry chuckled. "That's famous news!"

"Thank you for your approval," Barnaby said dryly, "but I would be obliged if you'd all turn round and make yourselves scarce. Unless, of course, you think it necessary to do *this* for me, too!"

"No, no," said Harry, whisking himself out.

"Wouldn't think of interfering," Terence murmured, following his brother out the door.

"Seems to me," said the Earl, backing to the door and cackling with delight, "that you're doing quite splendidly all on your own. Just as I always said you would."

· Epilogue ·

A YEAR LATER, rosy-cheeked from the cold and brimming with good spirits, Mr. and Mrs. Barnaby Traherne came into their town house on Henrietta Street from a Christmas frolic given by Molly Davenham. Barnaby took his wife's cloak from her shoulders, shook the snow from it and handed it, with his greatcoat, to the butler. Taking the fellow aside, he asked in an undervoice, "Is the job done, Merwin?"

"Yes, sir. Everything's in place," the butler whispered back. Then he threw Barnaby a half-smile and a wink and discreetly withdrew.

Miranda, crossing the foyer to the stairway, turned round. "Did you say something, dearest?"

Barnaby returned to her in three quick strides. "Just dismissing Merwin," he said, pulling her into his arms. "I've been waiting for hours to be alone with my bride."

She slipped her arms about his neck. "Scarcely a bride, my love. By this time next month, we shall be wed a whole year."

"A whole year!" He shook his head in disbelief. "I continue to feel as if we're still on our honeymoon." He kissed her mouth, his hand caressing her throat, the throat whose sensuous curves never failed to clench his innards. "Did you see how the Prime Minister devoured you with his eyes?" he murmured, his lips against hers. "I wanted to call the damned fellow out!"

Miranda giggled. "He was no worse than Celia Carew. The little minx flirted with you shamelessly."

"Did she indeed? I never noticed."

He let her go and, with arms about each other's waist, they started for the stairs. "Molly Davenham remarked to me that marriage has changed you drastically," Miranda said, throwing her husband a laughing glance.

"Drastically?" Barnaby's brows rose in surprise. "In what way?"

"She said you were no longer—" But she stopped in midsentence, for they were passing the sitting room doorway, and she had a fleeting impression that something within had been moved. For a moment, she thought she glimpsed a familiar piece of furniture: her old Sheraton desk. But of course, it couldn't be . . .

"No longer what?" Barnaby was asking.

She shook off her momentary lapse and grinned up at him. "Forbidding. She says you used to be forbidding."

"Nonsense," he retorted complacently, urging her up the stairs. "I was never forbidding. How can a fellow who suffered from a near-fatal case of shyness be called forbidding?"

They'd reached the top of the stairs. He dropped his hold on her, crossed the hallway and threw open their bedroom door. His eyes swiftly took in the scene before him. Merwin had done very well; the floral arrangement on the night table was perfect, and all the candles were lit.

Miranda came up behind him and blinked. For a moment she didn't breathe. Then she gasped, "My *bed*!" She crossed the threshold like one dazed and gaped at the huge four-poster ensconced against the far wall. "It's Mama's Queen Anne bed! How did you—?" She turned to her husband and threw herself into his arms. "*Barnaby*! How could you have known?"

Barnaby beamed down at her glowing face. "Your Aunt Letty told me about it, and about your desk, too. It's downstairs in the sitting room."

Miranda put a trembling hand to her forehead. "No, no, all this is quite impossible. How could you have talked to Aunt Letty? And how could you have persuaded Belle Velacott to give the pieces up? I'm dreaming."

"You're wide awake, my love, I promise you. Once your aunt told me the story, I had very little difficulty in persuading the Velacotts to return your property. In fact, they were so delighted to be invited to our anniversary ball, they were almost eager to part with the furniture."

"Anniversary *ball*? Wait a moment, please. You're going much too fast for me. First, when and where did you speak to Aunt Letty?"

"I went to see her last week."

"You went to see her?"

He nodded. "To invite her to our anniversary ball. You do want her here for that occasion, don't you?"

She gazed up at him with eyes that were beginning to brim with tears. "Are we going to have a *ball*? But I thought you disliked them."

"With you at my side, my dearest, I've discovered that they are quite enjoyable affairs. Don't you *want* to have a ball to celebrate our first year?"

"Oh, Barnaby!" She drew him down beside her on her newly-restored bed and, clutching him tightly round the waist, nuzzled his neck. "An anniversary ball is exactly what I want."

"Good, then. It's done. We shall have the grandest of balls and invite absolutely everyone. All my brothers. All their wives. Your aunt Letty. The Velacotts. Everyone in the world we've ever known. It shall be the most talked-about crush of the Season. There are only two requests I have to make of you in regard to it."

"Oh? And what are they?" she murmured contentedly.

"First, that you wear your green gown."

"Done. What else?"

He put his cheek against her hair and breathed in the fragrance of her. "That *this* time, my dearest, you give me the opportunity to sign your blasted dance card before it's filled."